A CHRISTMAS ENGAGEMENT

Adjusting to life without her late husband, Molly Reid is determined to make the most of a holiday to Madeira. As the dreamlike days of surf and sun pass, a friendship with her tour guide Michael develops and grows, though she wonders whether his attention and care are just part of his job. Back in Wales, meanwhile, Molly's daughter and son-in-law are hatching a surprise family reunion over Christmas — and it looks like the family could be about to gain some new members . . .

JILL BARRY

A CHRISTMAS ENGAGEMENT

Complete and Unabridged

LINFORD
Leicester

First published in Great Britain in 2014

First Linford Edition
published 2015

A catalogue record for this book is available
from the British Library.

ISBN 978–1–4448–2656–2

Published by
F. A. Thorpe (Publishing)
Anstey, Leicestershire

Set by Words & Graphics Ltd.
Anstey, Leicestershire
Printed and bound in Great Britain by
T. J. International Ltd., Padstow, Cornwall

This book is printed on acid-free paper

1

Sunshine and Reflection

'I hate hats, Mum!'

'I'd never have guessed,' said Tina. 'But if you want to go back in the paddling pool, you need to wear one or your hair might sizzle.'

Chuckling, Jack made a face and scampered off to join his sister just as Tina's mobile phone buzzed. Her mother, Molly, on holiday in Madeira, was soaking up the sun and looking forward to an indulgent hotel tea with someone in her tour group.

Tina swiftly replied to the text. *Have fun, Mum. It's pretty hot here in Wales too!*

In her mind's eye she pictured a table draped with snowy white cloth and set with dainty cucumber sandwiches and bite-size scones topped with clotted cream and strawberry jam. The silver cake stand would of course be spilling over with chocolate éclairs, miniature meringues and buttery sponge cakes. Such delicacies deserved eggshell-thin pretty china and an elegant silver teapot. Her mother had a thing about the art of brewing a decent cuppa. The leaves had to be Indian, of course, and nothing perfumed, however delicate the scent.

Tina felt pleased that Molly, on her first solo holiday, had found pleasant company. Afternoon tea, however scrumptious and luxurious, would surely taste better with someone there to share the experience.

A wail from inside the house pushed Tina to her feet. 'Sophie? Jack? Could you get out now, please? Your brother's awake.' She crossed the daisy-splashed lawn, big fluffy bath towel in hand, ready to spread on the grass. 'Hop on the magic carpet, you two. When I come back, you can tell me which lands you've flown to!'

From inside, Sam's wail grew louder

and more indignant as Tina hurried upstairs, thinking her younger son, at twelve months, often made more noise than the other two put together.

She pushed open the half-ajar door of the tiny bedroom. 'Sam! What's all this about? Mummy's here now, poppet.' He beamed at her. 'As if I'd forget you! Let's get you out of your cot.'

Tina lifted the warm boy-baby bundle into her arms for a cuddle. 'How about a nice, cool drink? Then we'll go outside for a few more minutes before tea.'

She walked carefully down the stairs and collected the well-used baby box. Outside, Sophie was instructing Jack where to steer the magic carpet. Currently they were in Lion Land but heading for a planet called Starfish. Sophie had recently become fixated on planets and stars. And starfish.

Sam thrust his chubby little arms above his head as his mum laid him on the black-and-white checked rug beneath the yellow parasol. The baby's hands always reminded her of starfish. Some time soon, she must organise a family trip to the seaside.

Tina thought of her mum again. It would be so wonderful if Molly could be a more hands-on grandma. But Molly lived in Cornwall. Gavin's parents had retired to Spain some years before. Families were so scattered these days. She sighed, secured Sam's nappy and picked him up, handing him his teddy-bear drinking cup.

Sophie and Jack ran across the grass. 'Can we have a drink, Mummy?' asked the former.

'Haven't you forgotten something?'

'I mean please! And you have to help us. Jack can't find the way to Planet Starfish.'

'Oh dear,' said Tina. 'We'll see if we can navigate our way there after tea, shall we?' She secured Sam in his baby seat. 'Let's get your sandals back on, you two. And Jack, I can't believe how filthy your hands are! Which planet did you visit to get so grubby?

Molly Reid settled into her soft cushioned wicker chair overlooking the Atlantic Ocean. Taking tea on this particular terrace was something she and her late husband had looked forward to doing, especially as their surname was the same as the name of this well-known hotel. She couldn't stop her lips twitching, remembering how her late husband used to joke about turning up at the desk and teasing the receptionist about being a long-lost family member. They'd never have afforded the room rates but at least she was here now, wearing a floral summer dress and her best strappy sandals — even though sitting with a woman she hardly knew and who, like herself, wasn't holidaying as part of a couple.

Their young waiter, flaxen hair tied in a ponytail, appeared from nowhere. 'Everything is all right, ladies?'

'Perfect, thanks,' said Kathy, Molly's holiday friend. 'Would you mind taking our photograph? My camera's ever so easy.'

The waiter positioned himself. 'Budge up, ladies please.'

Molly chuckled. 'Who's taught you English slang?'

'I have girlfriend,' said the young man, clicking once and then again. 'I have made sure of the ocean background.' He hurried off.

'Do you think they put dye in the ocean?'

Molly smiled. 'I know what you mean. That turquoise is unbelievable.'

'I could get used to this lifestyle though. What say you?'

'Being waited on? I'm not sure,' said Molly. 'It's probably like everything else in life. Too much rich food and we'd be longing for boiled egg and soldiers.'

Kathy sighed. 'Maybe, but I'm glad I booked this tour. And meeting up with you and not being a Johnny No-mates is an absolute bonus.'

'Same here.'

'Are you looking forward to the

group dinner later?' said Kathy. 'Even if the eligible males are in short supply.'

'Um, George is single, isn't he?' Privately Molly thought their fellow tour member must be at least twenty years older than Kathy.

'I was only having a laugh. Anyway, that widow from Brighton has her sights set on him. I can't believe how much lipstick she wears.' She gave Molly a knowing look. 'What do you think?'

'I think we should pay the bill and check out the ladies' washroom. If it's anything like the rest of this place, it's bound to be classy.'

Molly realised how right she was when they entered the luxurious ladies' room with its fluffy towels and upmarket soaps and hand creams. But she felt a sudden inexplicable pang of longing for her family as she and Kathy strolled back to the hotel's foyer. She'd booked for this tour many months before retiring from her office job. With more time on her hands, she'd stayed a while with her daughter and also visited her son

Tom and his wife, Lucy, up north.

But slowly, Molly's elderly neighbour's mobility problems had resulted in a few kind deeds and errands developing into a regular role. Her neighbour's family and all Molly's family and friends had insisted she must take full advantage of her holiday on the beautiful island of Madeira. But at that moment, she wished her children didn't live in opposite directions. Why did people have to scatter all over?

Things could be worse. At least neither of her offspring had moved to Australia. Molly dragged her thoughts back to the present as she and her companion wandered outside to explore the hotel grounds. Next day they planned to visit the Botanical Gardens. This was a dream holiday for Molly, someone passionate about gardening.

'We should take loads of photos,' said Kathy. 'They'll cheer us up on a dreary winter's evening.'

'Ooh!' Molly shuddered. 'You make it sound so depressing. Winter brings good things as well.'

'What, like Christmas?' Kathy stopped to sniff an exotic flower. 'What's this one called? Love the colours.'

'That's the Bird of Paradise. Very well-named, isn't it?'

Kathy seemed still fixated on winter. 'Hmm — good things like cuddly sweaters and fluffy slippers. Hot chocolate laced with brandy. And yes, of course the festive season. I've already stashed away a few gifts. You never know, I might buy the remaining ones while we're here.'

'Excuse me!' Molly laughed. 'Should we really be discussing Christmas? It comes round far too fast as it is.'

Kathy sank down on a wrought-iron bench. 'I love my family, but my mum and everyone always wants to come to my place and it's a huge amount of work for me. Worth it of course,' she added.

'No one ever wants to come to mine,' said Molly.

Kathy said nothing but she cleared her throat and fidgeted with her handbag strap.

'That came out all wrong,' said Molly. 'It's not that I'm a recluse! I told you I live in Cornwall, but I didn't say my son lives in Newcastle and my daughter in west Wales.'

'A bit of a trundle for all concerned?'

'Absolutely. Christmas isn't the ideal time for travelling long distances, and children always prefer being at home when Santa comes, don't they?'

'I think they want the right people round them,' said Kathy.

For once, Molly noticed a reflective expression on her companion's face. 'You know what?' she said. 'I think we should go back and take a siesta so we're nicely refreshed for tonight. What do you reckon?'

'Good idea. We could walk to the hotel through the park. The flowers are gorgeous and the tennis courts are always teeming.'

'How about stopping for a cool drink in that little café with the striped awning?' Molly got to her feet. 'When we get back, I think I'll have a quick swim before my rest. There'll be plenty of time before dinner.'

★   ★   ★

Molly enjoyed a quiet half hour in the hotel pool. Most of the guests were still out, some returning from the various excursions available. She'd already taken the one-day tour of the island's northern region and planned to see the other end of Madeira later that week.

Now she stood in front of the dressing-table mirror in her bedroom. She'd blown dry her dark brown hair and put on a sea-green dress with pretty ruched sleeves ending just above her elbows. She'd vowed not to wear tights on holiday and because she wore shorts for gardening on summer days, her legs weren't ghastly white as they were in winter. Molly had given up wearing high heels but her comfortable gunmetal pumps suited her outfit.

Her late husband would have liked this frock. But then he liked pretty well everything about her. She'd been very lucky. She still missed John terribly but knew he'd have hated her to sit at home, wallowing in loneliness.

She picked up her key card and slipped it into her bag. She was a little early but if she went down to the bar, she could grab a table ready for Kathy and anyone else on their own who might care to join her. Unless, of course, Michael the tour manager had decided to mix everyone up so they got a chance to chat to new people. That might be interesting. It was good for her to cope with new situations. To her amazement she began to feel the first pangs of hunger. How dare she, having demolished her share of such a superb tea earlier?

★ ★ ★

Peace at last. Tina cuddled baby Sam to her chest and took him upstairs. Already his dark eyelashes fluttered like little fans as he headed for the Land of Nod.

Gavin had got back early for once and taken over bath-time and the bedtime story for Sophie and Jack. But if Daddy added some extra details of his own to a favourite tale, he'd have Sophie to reckon with. Their daughter liked things to be the same and probably knew their favourite bedtime stories word for word.

Tina tiptoed away from the cot. She'd already drawn the yellow-and-white striped curtains. The mobile her mum had given her after Sophie's birth hung from the ceiling. The colourful carousel had done duty for the first two babies and its happy children riding cute ponies still delighted the latest addition to the family.

Downstairs in the kitchen, Tina helped herself to a glass of cider, the golden liquid fizzing into the tumbler as she poured. She glanced towards the kitchen door as her husband came through.

'Secret drinking?' He crossed the room and put his arms around her.

'Must have been a bad day!'

'Not at all. Anyway, isn't this one of my five a day? Hey, let me put the glass down!' Tina laughed as he took her in his arms. 'What's all this? Our wedding anniversary isn't for another fortnight.'

'I just wanted to prove I hadn't forgotten that little touch of romance.' He kissed her and let her go. 'I might have a glass of cider too. If I'd got here a little earlier, I could have started supper.'

'No problem. I took lasagne from the freezer this morning and the salad's chilling.' She smiled at him and perched on a stool at the breakfast counter.

'Why don't I cook the Sunday dins this weekend? Give you a bit of a break.' Gavin opened the fridge door and peered inside.

'Having you home in time to take Sophie and Jack off my hands is brilliant. Believe me.'

'You're a great mum. I just wish either of the grandmothers lived closer. Have you ever thought about speaking to Molly about moving?'

Tina stared at him. 'What, Mum or us, do you mean?'

'Molly, of course! We love it here, don't we?'

'Phew. You had me worried. Yes, west Wales is beautiful and you're settled in your job. So, has Mum said anything to you about moving?'

'Not in so many words.' He sat down opposite his wife. Then he winced, stood up again and held out a plastic brick. 'I didn't notice Jack's booby trap.'

Tina sipped her cider. 'Lethal when one turns up in your slipper.'

'I just wanted to say I think Molly's missing having family around more than she'll admit. Last time she visited — which is months ago now — she and I were washing up together and she hinted she felt undecided about her future.'

'What? She truly hasn't said a word to me, Gavin. Any idea what led her to make that comment?'

'She might have been tired. It's a heck of distance for her to drive on her own, don't forget.'

15

'I'm well aware of that. But she's always been independent. Always did her share of the driving. She insisted on keeping her job, even though Dad would've preferred her to retire when he did.'

'I think this caring role of hers is quite demanding. Your mum mentioned how it carved up her day. And sad though it may be, that situation's not going to get any better.'

'But Mum's not short of money, is she? She must want to go out to work, even if it's down the road to help out an old lady. And she has to shop for herself anyway. You know she can't be doing with online groceries.'

'I do.' Gavin shot Tina a mischievous grin. 'Will we ever forget the time she ordered six miniature tubes of toothpaste?'

'I don't know how she managed that.' Tina bit her lip. 'That was in the same delivery as the jumbo-sized bag of frozen spinach. She reckoned it took her two months to get through it.'

'We can all make mistakes.' Gavin

drained his glass. 'Has she been in touch from sunny Madeira?'

'I had a text to say she's enjoying herself. Found someone to knock about with, by the sound of things.'

'Great. I think we should be proud of her for having the confidence to go away with a lot of strangers. Just think, one day, I'll be able to take you away from all this and treat you to a holiday somewhere exotic.'

Tina chuckled. 'One day. For now, I'm perfectly happy as we are. But you've set me thinking about Mum. Maybe I'll ring my brother later. See if she's said anything to him.'

'When did she last visit Tom?'

'Oh heck, it must have been when Melissa turned two.'

'And Melissa is how old now — thirteen?'

'Very funny! You know she's coming up for three. But Tom and Lucy went down to Cornwall last Christmas, don't forget.'

'It's not so bad for them. Planning a

holiday, I mean. Teachers get more time for travel.'

'Don't tell Tom that. Teachers have stacks of preparation to do, don't they?'

'Oh, I wouldn't argue with that. Being a social worker and living where we do is very different though. You know how big an area I cover for work.'

'Well, Mum won't be planning any visits for a while, I reckon. She's not due back for another week and she won't want to set off again, much as I'd love to see her.'

'Hang on.' Gavin slithered off his stool and went into the hallway.

Tina held her breath. It was too much to hope none of the children would wake at some point.

He came back in, smiling. 'I can hear a little voice singing.'

'Jack?'

'Yep. I love our kids, Tina.'

'I know you do.'

'I'm wondering whether we could arrange a big, beautiful surprise for your Mum.'

18

'What sort of surprise?'

'How long is it since she had a proper, old-fashioned family Christmas?'

'Well, she had three of her family with her last year, don't forget.'

'Some of her family, yes. But how long since both you and Tom spent Christmas with her?'

Tina thought hard. 'Probably not since the year before my brother graduated. I was still living at home and my auntie and uncle came to stay. Yes, that was the last time, I reckon.'

'So how do you think she'd like it if we all got together this year? That way, she'd have her children, her daughter-in-law and son-in-law plus four grandchildren and her sister and husband, all within nagging distance at the same time.'

Tina laughed. 'You know very well Mum doesn't nag. But how on earth could we all fit into one house?' She counted on her fingers. 'That would make eleven of us — twelve if you count my cousin Dave. He always goes home to Auntie Helen's for Christmas if he's back in the UK.'

'I think the last time I saw him must've been Tom and Lucy's wedding. Nice guy. So, let's say we need accommodation for twelve assorted adults and little people?'

'Impossible. Even if we all went to Tom's and put the children in sleeping bags, can you imagine the chaos?' She shuddered. 'I don't think Tom could handle it, even if we all mucked in with the cooking.'

'Shall we eat? And while we tuck into that lovely homemade lasagne, I'll tell you how we can sort this whole matter out.'

★   ★   ★

Molly locked her room and headed for the lift. While gliding down to the ground floor, she anxiously checked her reflection again. The dim lighting made her look pale. Not the best of confidence-boosters. But when the door slid open and she stepped into the foyer, Lucas, her favourite waiter, happened to be passing.

'Senhora!' He beamed and said something incomprehensible.

'I'm sorry, Lucas, but I only know about four words of your lovely language.'

He lifted her hand to his lips. 'I tell you how beautiful you look this evening.'

She hadn't blushed for years but she felt warmth flood her cheeks. The young waiter had provided just the boost she needed, although he probably paid similar compliments to every mature lady guest. Her son would mutter something cynical about eyeing up his tip!

'Thank you,' she said. 'Um, *obrigado*?'

'Yes, yes. Very good, but you not need to thank me. Go and enchant your companions. Enjoy your evening, senhora.'

Her son and daughter, thought Molly as she headed for the bar, would really fall about laughing. And there was that little pang again. Being abroad, dressing for dinner, spending time with a load of strangers, was all very well. It had taken

21

courage for her to book a holiday for herself, even within the confines of an escorted group. But at that moment she'd have exchanged it all if she could be whisked away to Wales or Newcastle. For the hundredth time, she wished her offspring didn't live in such far-flung places.

'Hello, Mrs Reid. You're the first here.'

She smiled at Michael, their tour guide. 'I'm known for being annoyingly punctual, Mr Todd. You must have noticed by now.'

'It's a quality to be admired. But please, you must call me Michael.'

'Only if you call me Molly.'

'It's a deal. Now, there's a glass of champagne on the house if you'd like to come this way.'

Molly followed Michael across the dark red carpet and accepted a glass of bubbly from the smiling barman.

'I have to meet and greet,' said Michael. 'But maybe we'll have a chance to chat later. I have a scheme to mix everyone around so we don't sit with the same table companions all evening. I hope no one minds.'

'I shouldn't think so,' said Molly. 'This is a very friendly crowd.'

'I can't remember when I had a nicer group. Now here comes George, so you'll have some company.'

Molly watched as George collected his drink and to her surprise made a beeline for her.

'May I join you? It's Mrs Reid, isn't it?'

'Please do. And it's Molly. I was just saying to Michael how annoyingly punctual I am.'

'I have the same problem.' George looked down at his glass. 'Are we supposed to drink this now, or wait until everyone's here?'

'Oh, I think we should make the most of the bubbles. But I'll make this one last. Don't want to wake up tomorrow with a hangover.'

'Are you booked on an excursion?'

'No. Two of us are sharing a taxi to

the Botanical Gardens.'

'You'll enjoy that. I've been several times.'

'Already?'

'Only once this trip, but my late wife and I loved coming here. We used to rent a villa at Santa Cruz. The area's become more commercialised over the years of course, but we enjoyed being so close to the ocean.' He shot her a wistful smile.

'How lovely that must have been. I expect you treasure many happy memories.'

'Oh yes.' He glanced at her wedding ring. 'I mustn't pry, but as you're travelling on your own, so to speak . . . '

'I'm a widow. It's weird becoming suddenly single, don't you think?'

He nodded his head. 'Still not used to it, to be honest. But we have to get on with life, don't we? Our other halves wouldn't have wanted us to sit home alone and brood.'

'Are you a keen gardener?'

George's eyes lit up. Molly, listening

as he described the layout of his garden back home, didn't notice her new friend enter the room a few paces behind the lively widow who Kathy thought wore too much lipstick.

George leaned across the table. 'I'm so glad to make your acquaintance. I have to confess the lady over there in the pink dress — the one who's just come in — seems determined to monopolise me. I can't for the life of me think why. If she joins us, please don't leave me!'

Molly grinned. 'I promise to protect you.' She beckoned to Kathy. 'Safety in numbers. You'll enjoy Kathy's company, and I promise she won't monopolise you.'

Gradually, the thirty-two tour members filled the room with laughter and chatter. Molly wondered how on earth Michael would gain everyone's attention as the time for the group's gala dinner drew close. But he strode to the centre of the room and clapped his hands.

'Ladies and gentlemen, this evening

is a chance for you to talk to people you mightn't yet have met properly. You don't all choose the same excursions and you eat at different times. So, sit where you wish for now, but I shall ask all the gentlemen to move around three places to their left, between main course and dessert. Enjoy your dinner, everyone.'

Molly, Kathy and George sat at one of the two big round tables prepared for the holidaymakers. Molly chose the seafood starter, followed by a local speciality, beef grilled on a spit of laurel. During the lull before dessert was served, sure enough, Michael reminded the gentlemen to rise and move the requested three places to the right. To Molly's surprise, it was the tour guide who claimed George's vacant chair and sat down beside her.

'Lovely food,' she said, feeling a little light-headed after the sparkling wine and unaccustomed rich meal.

'Yes, this hotel's one of my favourites,' said Michael.

Molly hesitated. 'Do you ever tire of travelling? Yours sounds like a dream job, but don't your family miss you?'

He shook his head.

'Goodness, I'm sorry,' said Molly. 'I think that champagne has loosened my tongue. I'm not usually so tactless.'

'Don't worry. It's something I'm asked a lot. But I'm on my own and both my daughters lead busy lives. So far there are no grandchildren. If that should happen, I might reconsider and retire.'

Molly thought he looked a little wistful. 'I know just what you mean. I do have grandchildren — four altogether. But both my son and my daughter live too far away for me to see much of either of them.'

'Would you ever consider moving, Molly? At least you'd end up closer to one of them.'

'I've thought about it,' she said. 'But I have my friends and my lovely garden. I could uproot myself and move over to Wales or go all that way up to

Newcastle, and a couple of years down the line find Tom, or Tina's husband, upping sticks because of promotion or whatever.'

'So, do you do any volunteering or much travelling?'

Molly realised, to her surprise, she hadn't mentioned her caring role. 'I keep an eye on an elderly lady. It began as a good neighbour kind of thing but her daughter asked me if we could put things on a regular basis. I booked this holiday before I left my office job and started my caring duties, so here I am.'

'Here come the desserts,' said Michael. 'What did you order?'

Molly chuckled. 'Madeira cake with whipped cream. I'll probably break the lift when I go upstairs.'

'I doubt that. I chose the passion fruit pudding. I'll need to take a brisk walk later.'

'Well, if you'd like some company, I could do with a walk too, though I managed a swim today.'

'I'm impressed,' said Michael. 'And

yes, I'd appreciate your company. Tour guides spend a fair amount of time being amongst people but not with them, if you know what I mean.'

2

Destination Christmas

'But wouldn't it cost an absolute fortune? Can you show me the kind of house you mean on the laptop?'

While Gavin fired up the computer, Tina rose and stretched. 'I'll just go and check on the babies.'

When she came back, her husband pointed out the image of a large house. She pulled her chair closer.

'There are plenty of properties big enough to take twelve or fourteen people,' Gavin said. 'Remember we rented that tiny cottage in Cornwall when you were expecting Sophie? That was at the other end of the scale.'

'Bijou, as they say, but really great. We spent time with my folks but came and went as we pleased. That didn't cost an arm and a leg though. Unlike this place, beautiful though it looks.'

'You're not thinking straight, Tina. If we can get your brother interested, and your aunt and uncle and cousin, and we split the bill among us, it won't be that horrendous. When did you and I last have a proper holiday?'

'Um, that time in Cornwall?'

'Exactly. We've had loads of lovely times with the kids on the beach and we're lucky to live not too far from the coast. But this would be an opportunity for the lot of us to get together. We'd all have to do our bit, but imagine how fantastic it'd be.'

'Mum would be in seventh heaven.'

'If we don't arrange a reunion soon, the little ones will grow up hardly knowing their own close relatives. Think about it.'

Molly stared at the screen. 'Where is this place?'

'That one's in Somerset. I'm using it just to show you the kind of properties available. But if you like the idea, one of us should run it past Tom and Lucy.

It'd be great to spend time with them. I'm fond of them too, remember.'

Tina rose and stood behind her husband, winding her arms around his shoulders and snuggling her cheek next to his. 'It's a brilliant idea, love. But where would we choose to stay? There'll still be long distances to cover.'

'I already have a couple of suggestions, but we should wait and see what the others think before going further.'

'I don't expect it'll be all sweetness and light,' said Tina. 'Christmas is the time when couples have been known to fight, isn't it?'

Gavin swivelled in his chair and pulled his wife onto his knee. 'If you start getting antsy, I shall make you wrap up warm and go out for a hike.'

'Okay.' She giggled. 'As long as I have permission to do the same to you!'

'Now, who's going to ring Tom and Lucy and who's going to wash up?'

'Why don't you make the call? I can have a word after you've spoken to Tom.'

'Hmm,' said Gavin. 'I'm happy to ring but I hope he won't think I'm interfering.'

'I'm sure he won't. Knowing my big brother, he'll be calculating the most convenient meeting point, even if it's halfway up a mountain.'

★   ★   ★

Tom Reid pushed the pile of work-sheets he'd been examining into a neat square and tucked them into his briefcase. His laptop was already up and running, so he typed the name Gavin had provided into the search engine and felt a surge of excitement.

His wife was babysitting a friend's two children while Tom caught up with his marking. Before she returned, he wanted to do his own research regarding his brother-in-law's startling but tempting idea.

Tom's logical mind had already begun calculating the most convenient places for a family rendezvous. He liked the idea very much, although the weather could be a problem at that time of year. His fingers flew as he checked out possibilities. Gavin and Tina would drive. He and Lucy would too. But would his mother be keen to travel such a distance on her own? Suddenly the possibility occurred to him that if she took a train to Bristol, Gavin and Tina could pick her up.

Aunt Helen and Uncle Richard didn't live far from London, so they'd have lots of transport options. How long was it since he'd seen them? Could it have been his own wedding day, or was it another, far more poignant family event? In either case, Lucy had hardly exchanged more than a few words with the couple. It was a shame how people so dear to him, so important in his childhood days, had dwindled into names to be ticked off on a Christmas card list. Tom made a note of another possible area. He was looking at motorway routes from Bristol, Newcastle, and London. This was the interesting bit for him and a challenge he enjoyed.

He heard Lucy's key in the lock. The house was quiet, with Melissa sleeping the sleep of the exhausted toddler. He got up to welcome his wife back. 'So, did the terrible twins behave?'

She put her bag down and gave him a hug. 'Eventually. I think they must have tried every trick in the book known to nine-year-olds. I wouldn't let them play computer games, so they got their own back by asking me to read to them.'

'Well, that's good, isn't it?' Tom moved across to fill the kettle.

'Of course. Was Melissa OK?'

'Yep. And I had a long conversation with Gavin and Lucy.'

'Aw, I'm sorry I missed them. Anything in particular?'

'Tea? Then I can tell you all about it.'

Lucy sat down at the table. When Tom brought their mugs over, he shot her a guilty look, and headed to the fridge for the chocolate biscuits. 'Week-ends only, we decided!' he said.

'Please miss, can we break the rules? Just this once?'

'Any particular reason?'

'Only that I need a clear head to work out something.'

Tom explained the Christmas project to his wife. Lucy raised her eyebrows but listened quietly as he talked about the practicalities.

'Problem is,' he said, 'would your mum and dad be offended if we took off for the festive period? We usually go to them — except for that one year we went to my mother's.'

'I'm sure they'd understand,' said Lucy. 'After all, they see a lot of Melissa. I'd really miss help with childcare. It probably wouldn't be worth doing my three days a week of hairdressing without Mum taking over.'

'We're lucky having them close and handy,' said Tom. 'I often wonder how the heck my sister copes with three little ones. Gavin's job is very demanding.'

'Tina's very calm; she takes after your mother. But I know Molly misses seeing her grandchildren.'

'Yes, well, I've had that discussion with her before. There's nothing to stop her moving nearer Tina and Gavin, or us for that matter.'

'She values her friends, Tom, especially now she's on her own. And she has her little job.'

'A little job that's escalated into a big responsibility. She daren't go away even for a couple of days without giving notice in triplicate.'

'It's her life, Tom. And from what Tina says, that elderly lady's family think the world of your mum. One day she might decide to move closer to us or to Tina and I'm sure we'll all rally round.'

'So you're OK with this idea? All of us converging on one big house for — how many days would it be?'

'Wouldn't we have to book for a week? That's quite a long time.'

He chuckled. 'Chickening out already?'

Lucy whisked the chocolate biscuits from under his nose. 'Two's plenty.

Biscuits, I mean, not days! Of course I'm not chickening out. It'll do Melissa good to be with her cousins. Sophie will love being the big girl and Melissa will adore baby Sam.'

'Jack's my favourite.'

'Yes, well remember it's only because of Skype that we get to talk to him.'

'At least that keeps us all in touch. Even Mum's stopped being suspicious about computers since we persuaded her to have a laptop.'

'So which areas do you reckon we should consider?'

'I've written a few down.' He passed her his notepad. 'So, what do you think? Tina and Gavin are doing the same and we'll pool our suggestions and hopefully agree on a destination.'

'Destination Christmas! Girly chats with Tina over a bottle of wine while Mum enjoys her grandchildren and Auntie Helen gets to know her great-nieces and nephews better.'

'If we could find a place with an indoor swimming pool and games room, it would be the icing on the cake. A golf course nearby would be good too.'

'Unless of course . . . ' Lucy paused.

'Unless what?'

'Had you considered the possibility of a white Christmas?'

He laughed. 'We'll be going south. The aim is to meet roughly in the middle of our weird quadrangle, though I've changed that to a triangle by routing Mum's journey partly by rail.'

'Snow might still happen, whichever part of the country we're in. But if it did, it'd be magical.'

'It'd be a right pain, you mean.'

'So we won't talk about it. Oh dear, Tom, motorway links don't mean much to me. Can you redo your list in English, please? Counties even?'

⋆   ⋆   ⋆

Molly and her companion had arranged to meet in the foyer. Kathy already stood in reception, browsing the tourist leaflets. She looked up as Molly approached.

'I didn't see you at breakfast. Mind you, the lipstick lady didn't turn up either.'

'I was an early bird.'

'Did you enjoy last night? You got to sit next to George as well as Michael, you flirt!'

Molly chuckled. 'Sheer chance. I'm not looking for romance, Kathy. If I were, I'd have booked on one of those singles holidays.' She made a face.

'I went on one of those last year.'

'Whoops. Trust me to put my big foot in it.'

'No, not at all. I have to admit there were mostly women in the group. It was OK though. Lovely hotel on a Greek island.'

'I know you have children, but are you single, Kathy? If you don't mind my asking.'

'Divorced, but I don't mind telling you I met my new partner through online dating.'

'Wow, you're very brave. I truly don't think I could do that.'

'We're all different. This is early days for my new friend and me and I'd already booked my holiday when I first got to know him, but we're keeping in touch and he's collecting me from Gatwick. We'll take it from there.'

'I hope all goes well for you.'

'We must exchange addresses and so on. Then I can keep you posted and you can tell me how you're getting on with life.'

'I'd like that,' said Molly. 'Now, shall we make a move?'

'Don't look now, but lipstick lady's just getting out of the lift. Wearing a huge pair of shades!' She pulled a wry face. 'I did warn her to drink lots of water with her wine last night.'

'I hope she's not lonely behind those dark glasses. Should we ask her if she wants to join us?'

'You're such a kind person, Molly. But she told me she's booked on an excursion today. Let's check on taxis with the desk in case there's some kind of etiquette as to which one we choose.'

Outside, the two found no shortage of cab drivers, all eager for custom and all pleading theirs was the best, most comfortable taxi on the island. But Molly strode to the first in the queue. The driver jumped out and opened both rear doors.

'We'd like to go to the Botanical Gardens, please,' said Kathy.

'With very great pleasure, ladies. You've chosen a perfect day to visit a perfect location. Most days is perfect on our island,' said the driver.

They chatted with him about the areas they'd already visited and their journey didn't take long. Molly told him she planned to walk the levadas, the narrow channels transporting water from the mountains down to the dry, warmer south of the island. He impressed upon them the need to take great care and not to venture for their first time without the help of a guide.

'Doing our tour guide out of a job?'

Kathy nudged Molly.

'I'm sure Michael has enough to do already.'

'Well, you should know.'

'Sorry?'

'I'm only teasing you, Molly.'

But the throwaway remark set Molly wondering if people, even Kathy, suspected every single woman traveller of being a husband-hunter. It certainly wasn't true in her case, but probably not worth making a statement about.

'I wonder if there's a recommended route.' Kathy peered at one of the many leaflets she carried round in an enormous red raffia shoulder bag.

'We can wander round to our heart's content,' said Molly.

'Shall we stay together?'

'I'm happy with that,' said Molly. 'But in case we become separated, why don't we arrange a place to meet for morning coffee?'

It was Kathy who became diverted and got left behind, focusing her camera while she coaxed a parrot to speak to her. Molly wasn't too thrilled about seeing caged birds and she explored the paths, tackled the slope down into the giant fern garden and revelled in the cool, cathedral-like atmosphere. She surfaced to gaze at exotic flowers in hot shades of pink and orange as well as creamy camellias.

She had to hurry in order not to be late and found the café buzzing with customers, though luckily she noticed Kathy claiming a table just vacated. When they had their coffees, her new friend surprised Molly.

'You know, I envy you.'

'Whatever for?'

'You have a kind of serenity. I haven't heard one moan out of you and we got talking on Day One, don't forget. I'm always finding something to whinge about, even on this beautiful island.'

'I've had to become used to living alone and getting on with things. I'd be no use to myself or anyone else if I kept getting wound up.'

'I have two teenagers at home,' said

Kathy. 'Maybe I moan about them too much. Perhaps you'll become my role model.'

Molly laughed and banged her cup down on the saucer. 'My Americano almost went down the wrong way. Don't think I don't do my share of complaining. I think, as we become older, we're a wee bit prone to make comparisons. Our younger lives look rosier than maybe they actually were.'

Kathy nodded.

'I can't help wondering why you chose this holiday,' said Molly. 'You're definitely the youngest person in the group.'

'I love islands and I didn't want to be somewhere noisy. This is perfect.'

'Well, I'm glad you're here.'

'Thanks, but you're such a friendly person, you'd always find someone to keep you company.'

Molly thought how much she'd enjoyed talking to Michael the evening before but daren't risk being teased.

'So, do you see much of your family?'

Kathy asked. 'You mentioned your son and daughter. Do you have grandchildren?

'Four altogether — two boys and two girls, all under seven years of age.' Molly leaned forward. 'To be honest, I'm feeling guilty about being here on holiday. I could have gone to stay with each of my children in turn, instead of whizzing off abroad.'

'So, why didn't you?'

'Good question. My late husband and I always planned to visit Madeira but didn't get round to it. That made me determined to see it before I got too ancient. You need to be fit to cope with all the slopes.'

'You're doing brilliantly. I'm only 43 and I have a job to keep up with you sometimes.' Kathy patted her middle. 'The result of comfort eating! It's coming down, slowly but surely.'

'That's by far the best way to lose weight,' said Molly. 'Nothing too drastic.'

'So will your children come to stay

with you in the school hols?'

'I should arrange something, I know, but I live near an old lady who's becoming more and more reliant on my help. Her daughter's found someone to stand in for me while I'm on holiday, but my time just melts away these days.'

'You sound regretful. People like you are invaluable, but just at the point when you could spend more time with your family, you've taken on this responsibility and it won't become any easier. You're torn.'

Molly stared at Kathy. That was exactly how she felt. Torn. 'One half of me wants to give notice that I can no longer cope with the demands of being a carer. The other half tells me that one day I might be in need of . . . of . . . '

'In need of someone like you?'

'You've got it.' Molly glanced up. 'There's that nice couple we talked to last night. They might like to share our table.' She beckoned. 'Thanks for listening. You see, I can moan when I've a mind.'

'I wouldn't call that a moan. I'd call you one very special lady.'

★   ★   ★

At the weekend, Tina, who'd fixed an appointment to Skype with her brother, switched on the laptop, feeling a little nervous. What if they were taking on something too complicated to arrange?

'I'm so glad someone invented this system,' she said as Gavin brought the baby into the kitchen. Sophie and Jack were colouring in with crayons while they waited to talk to their aunt and uncle.

'Our children take it for granted. When we were at school, we never even dreamt of being able to talk to anyone like this, across the miles.'

'Mum's fascinated by it.' Tina chuckled. 'She's become a Skye groupie.'

'Yep. She's really taken to her laptop. I thought she'd run a mile when we presented it to her but she couldn't wait to get started.'

'Okay, they're online now.' Tina waved to little Melissa, who sat on her mum's lap, staring solemnly at her auntie.

'How did you get on with your research?' Tom asked.

'Not too badly,' said Tina. 'You have your notebook, I see.'

'We've found three possibilities.'

'Snap! We've pared our suggestions down from seven,' said Gavin.

'What have you two gone for as basic requirements?' Lucy waved her daughter's fluffy blue rabbit at little Sam.

Tina took a deep breath. 'Obviously somewhere with enough bedrooms, plus a cot and spare folding beds. Oh, and a high chair.'

'En-suite accommodation seems pretty much standard,' said Lucy. 'So no queuing for the bathroom.'

'And if a house has the right number of bedrooms, we can guarantee the kitchen's big enough, even if a few of us might have to sit at a breakfast bar.'

'Okay,' said Lucy. 'What about the

luxury touches? Is it worth splurging, given this'll probably be a once in a lifetime event?'

'Definitely worth forking out for an indoor pool,' said Tom.

'We agree,' said Tina. 'Even if it's a small one.'

'The houses we've chosen are all in good walking country.'

'There must be a utility room for all those pairs of wellies,' said Tina. 'With a washing machine and tumble dryer, in case Gavin and Tom get their clothes muddy when they're out hiking.'

Gavin tweaked a tendril of Tina's fair hair and rolled his eyes at his brother-in-law. 'We'll try not to be too much trouble, won't we, Tom?'

'Speak for yourself.' Tom chuckled. 'So why don't we swap details and get back to each other?'

'Fine by us,' said Gavin, as Tina nodded approval.

'Tina, do you think you should be the one to tell Mum's big sister what we're planning? Helen mightn't fancy the idea, in which case we need to deduct three people from our list.'

'I'll try Auntie Helen now, if you like.' She called to her two elder children. 'Come and sit in my seat, Sophie and Jack, while I make a phone call.'

Helen answered after the second ring and lost no time telling Tina she'd already received a postcard from Madeira.

'Goodness, that was quick,' said Tina. 'She's sent text messages but no postcard yet.'

Helen laughed. 'Your mum knows I collect them. She probably posted mine soon after she landed. How are you all, anyway?'

'Fine, thanks. I'm ringing to say we're plotting a surprise for Mum and wonder if you and Uncle Chris would like to join in a family holiday? And Dave of course, if he's between contracts for Christmas.'

'What? Tina, I've barely begun wearing summer clothes.'

'If we want to get our first choice, it's not too soon to book.' Tina quickly explained. 'We'd love to do Christmas with all of us together for once. And it'd mean a lot to everyone, especially Mum, if you three could join us.'

'I love the idea,' said Helen. 'Chris is watching golf on TV at the moment and I probably won't get much sense out of him. Personally I'd rather watch paint dry.'

Tina smiled to herself. Her aunt would get round to something more positive before long.

'So how about I text you as soon as he surfaces?'

'That's fine. So I may tell the others you approve in principle?'

'Please do. Have you decided yet where we'd all be staying?'

'We're still at the research stage so if you want to join us, we'll send Uncle Chris the website links. I know you don't like emailing.'

'I'm old-fashioned, I know and there always seems something better to do with my time. But Chris can show me what you've found. I'm feeling excited already! It seems ages since I saw you all.'

'Exactly,' said Tina. 'We'll hope to hear from you soon. Oh, and Auntie Helen, if Mum happens to ring, remember not to breathe one single word of this conversation.'

She walked back into the kitchen and heard her husband tell the others he could see a smile upon her face.

'Helen sounded thrilled to bits,' said Tina, putting her head close to her daughter's. 'She's going to let me know what Uncle Chris thinks, so hopefully I can text you later.'

'If they're up for it, they'll need our suggestions too,' said Tom. 'Fingers crossed then, guys!'

'I'd better go,' said Lucy. 'Sorry, but one little girl's getting very restless. Bedtime calls. Speak to you soon.'

Tina blew a kiss. 'We'll be in touch.'

Before long, all three households had details of the six properties. Television programmes were forgotten in Gavin and Tina's house as they explored Shropshire, Worcestershire, the Cotswolds and Warwickshire. Everyone agreed good motorway connections were vital, in case the weather played up.

Two properties offered a small, heated swimming pool and another featured a hot tub, showing a family sitting in it, enjoying candle-lit quality time. Several houses were pet-friendly which, Tina decided, might well influence the decision for her aunt and uncle, who had a much-loved Border Collie. One property very much appealed to her and when she shared her thoughts with Gavin, he agreed too.

'Don't forget this is a joint decision, love,' he said to her when they grabbed a few minutes of relaxation on their patio, watching a beautiful blood-orange sunset.

His wife smiled. 'I'll keep an open mind. But it'd be wonderful if the others felt the same.'

'We also need a second choice to fall

back on if our first preference is already booked.'

Tina pulled a face. 'I hadn't thought of that, but of course there'll be lots of families thinking like we are.'

'Not only British ones either,' said Gavin. 'Though why we're not planning on jetting off to the sunshine, I really don't know.'

Tina stared at him. 'It honestly hadn't occurred to me to suggest it. I like the thought of piling everything into the car and being able to stop when and where we want.'

'Plus we won't have to worry about excess baggage and flight delays.' Gavin pointed upwards. 'Look at that sky now. It seems odd to have Christmas on our minds when we're barely past the summer solstice.'

Tina pulled her woolly cardigan around her shoulders, knotting the arms in front of her. 'There's more red and purple taking over the pinks and oranges now. We live in such a beautiful spot — it's a pity we can't entertain everyone here for Christmas.'

Gavin laughed. 'It's a lovely thought, but I don't think they'd appreciate camping on the lawn in December. So, do you want me to look at properties in our part of Wales? It's not too late.'

'No, love,' said Tina. 'It wouldn't be fair on the others, having to drive so far. Let's leave things as they are and wait to see what the others think.'

'Hang on,' said Gavin. 'Wouldn't it be a good idea to text Molly and ask her to keep Christmas free?'

'And spoil the surprise?'

'Maybe you could say we'd very much like her to spend Christmas with us and we're getting in first with our invitation. You never know. She's on holiday with a load of people and she's making new friends; they might decide to arrange a reunion. Such things have been known to happen.'

His wife picked up her phone. 'Good thinking, Batman. I'll text her straightaway.'

3

A Dawning Attraction

After dinner, Molly opted to sit on the hotel terrace and catch up with the paperback she'd hardly opened. A few of the other tour members decided to go for a stroll down town and watch the locals going about their evening, and she could see Kathy was keen to join them.

'I'm happy to be on my own. Off you go and hit the town!'

She was nursing a glass of lemonade and staring into the distance when she noticed a movement in the doorway through to the bar. But the moment Molly waved at their tour guide, she immediately felt embarrassed in case Michael thought she assumed he was seeking her company. Her sudden feeling of insecurity came too late, because he was weaving his way through the tables towards her.

'May I join you?'

'Of course, but please don't feel obliged to sit with me, Michael.'

She felt her cheeks warming and hoped, in the gentle glow of solar lighting, that no one, especially him, would notice her blushing. She couldn't help thinking it was a bit like being a teenager again. The poor fellow was merely doing his job. But not for the first time, she couldn't help thinking how kind his blue eyes were and how attractively the corners crinkled when he smiled.

He put down his glass opposite hers and pulled out a wicker chair.

'How did your day go? You were off to the Botanical Gardens, if I remember rightly.' He sat back and smiled at her.

'Kathy and I spent several hours there. It was amazing, especially for someone like me who loves gardening. For two pins I'd go back, but there's so much more of the island to see. Did you have a good day?'

'All went well. One of my charges was wearing a sundress but I assumed she'd packed a cardigan in the enormous bag she carried with her. I could have sworn I advised everyone to bring something warm ready for when we climbed higher up the mountain.'

'She must have been freezing at that altitude. I was grateful for the advice when I did that trip the other day. I made Kathy go back to her room for a woolly, otherwise she'd have been in the same boat.'

'The climate here in Funchal is so wonderful, I'm not surprised people are lulled into a false sense of security. Anyway, I noticed the lady's husband didn't offer her his jacket after we left the coach, so she promptly went off and bought a sweater from one of the craft stalls.'

'The stall holder must have been pleased to make a sale.'

'The sweaters are excellent quality, and she seemed pleased too.' He hesitated. 'You were looking very thoughtful before I arrived and interrupted your tranquillity. I hope all's well at home.'

'No problems. At least, if there are, no one's mentioned them. It's just that I've received an odd text message.'

'Dare I ask in what way it's odd?'

'My daughter's sent me a Christmas invitation! It's still June and I can't help wondering what all the urgency's about.' She felt a sudden chill. 'Oh my goodness, I hope one of them hasn't received some awful diagnosis.'

'Hey, come on now. That seems highly unlikely. Have you not considered maybe your daughter's missing you?'

'Well I miss her too. But surely it's strange to send me an invitation while I'm away on holiday? It's only June, so why not wait until I return?'

Michael pursed his lips. 'Perhaps she and your son-in-law are afraid someone on the tour will snap you up and invite you to their home for Christmas.'

Molly couldn't believe what she heard. 'Goodness, does that kind of thing often happen?'

He took a sip of his drink. 'Sometimes. You're a very pleasant lady, and often friendships are forged on holidays like this.'

Molly shook her head. 'I can't imagine accepting an invitation from someone I hardly know. But I'd be touched, I suppose.'

'Well, looks like you won't have to wonder where to spend the festive season this year.'

'I suppose not. I wish I had the space to invite both my son and daughter and their families to stay in Cornwall, but there's no way we could squeeze everyone in.'

'Sounds like you could do with a six-bedroom manor house.'

'I wish! But that's not likely to happen. I expect I'll find out why my daughter's so anxious to think about Christmas, after I return home.'

'In the meantime you still have lots of

holiday left. So, are you looking forward to tomorrow? If I remember rightly, you and your friend are booked on the full-day levadas walk.'

'Yes. We don't spend every single hour together, but I'm enjoying having someone to sit with for meals and when we go in different directions, it's good to compare notes at the end of the day.'

'You're the perfect tour member, Molly.'

'I don't know about that!' She chuckled. 'We have a local guide tomorrow, don't we?'

'Indeed you do. It makes for a better, safer experience, if there's someone with detailed knowledge of the area. Where you'll be walking is magical, especially if you enjoy waterfalls. The ground's a mass of ferns in places and there are tiny lakes as well as the beautiful cascades. You'll enjoy it.'

'I'm sure. We'll be glad of a teahouse stop to keep us going, I imagine.'

'You'll certainly have that.'

'It's strange how time seems to pass

more slowly here. In a good way, though. At home, my day's dominated by the clock.' She knew she must sound wistful.

'Well, let's hope you return refreshed and relaxed. As for me, it's off to the mountains again in the morning.' He rose as Molly gathered her handbag and paperback together.

She wished him goodnight and left him to enjoy the rest of his drink. Maybe she'd better respond to Tina's text when she reached her room. But she wasn't one hundred percent certain what that response should be.

The lift stopped on the fourth floor and Molly stepped out and headed to her room, still wondering what stopped her from answering her daughter's invitation with a big YES PLEASE!!! But by the time she sat down on the bed and called up the message, she knew exactly what she wanted to say. When Tina picked up her mother's response, she'd look at those four words and wonder what was going on. But at that moment, saying *we need to talk* seemed much the best option.

★ ★ ★

'What's that supposed to mean, I wonder.' Tina frowned at her phone.

'Sorry? I was on the side of a cliff, clinging on for dear life.' Gavin looked up from his book.

'Mum's answered my text. She says, and I quote, *We need to talk*. I thought she'd be pleased with our invitation. What am I supposed to do now?'

'Come to bed, love. Maybe you caught her at a bad moment.'

'She should be back in her room by now, surely.'

Gavin burst out laughing. 'What, are you your mother's keeper? Molly's on holiday. Maybe they're all having drinks with the tour manager or whatever.'

'It's not a cruise, Gav.' Tina settled herself beside him. 'It's the kind of package tour designed for the more mature traveller.'

'Which doesn't automatically mean lights out at ten p.m.' He stopped to think. 'Are they an hour behind us over there? Or have I got it the wrong way round?'

'The time in Madeira is exactly the same as here.'

'So, she's enjoying herself. She won't be woken at the crack of dawn by the thunder of little feet. She wants to live in the moment and not waste her summer holiday thinking about Christmas. That's fine. She'll be back before you know it and you can sort things out then, hopefully without giving away our plan.'

'I worry about her, though. She's bound to feel a bit strange, taking a holiday on her own after years of being one half of a couple. You know how close she and Dad were. She's probably still disorientated even though she puts a good face on things.'

Gavin abandoned his book and hugged his wife to him. 'Yes, they were a wonderful couple and fortunate enough to have several decades of happiness together. But now Molly has to pick up the pieces and adjust to being single instead of one half of a pair. Maybe you don't see things like I do, but I happen to think she's making a brilliant job of it. You know your father would be proud of her. You worry too much, love.'

Tina sighed. 'I expect you're right. Am I being over-protective?'

'Just a tad. Now, shall we call it lights out? Leave the partying to your mum and the rest of the silver surfers.'

Tina wished she could be as relaxed as her husband. Maybe it was all to do with his social worker experience. He was faced with all kinds of traumas during the course of his working day and she knew he was virtually unshockable. He'd seen the way bereavement unhinged people — rocked their comfort, their security and their whole way of life. Luckily, no way was her mum unhinged. Gavin was right in saying how well Molly coped.

But she lived miles away in Cornwall and there she was, choosing to spend her precious holiday time on the island of Madeira. Molly was an attractive lady, pleasant and easy company. What if some lonely widower or divorcé took a liking to her and turned on the charm? Worse still, what if this potential threat to her mum actually lived on the island? She'd be even further away from them than she was already. Surely her mother wouldn't allow such a thing to happen? But she knew Gavin was right to say she mustn't try and influence Molly's life.

Tina closed her eyes tight and snuggled under the duvet. It sounded as though her husband was already asleep. If she didn't reach the Land of Nod soon, a little voice would be telling her it was time to get up.

★   ★   ★

Molly's travel alarm beeped just as she reached out to switch it off. Sun streamed through the flower-splashed curtains, bringing the promise of another warm day on the island. Madeira's sub-tropical climate suited her and she liked the idea of living somewhere with virtually no extremes of temperature. She loved Cornwall and she'd lived there for twenty years but last winter, only the second on her own, and when she seemed all fingers and thumbs when lighting the wood-burner, she'd thought longingly of wintering away from the UK.

She'd left her mobile phone to charge all night. Guiltily, she remembered the text she'd sent. But there were no more messages so Tina must have taken her at her word. If only she lived near her daughter, she'd be able to help with childcare. Maybe Tina could get a part-time job then. After all, Sophie was at primary school and Jack went to nursery, but their grandma's babycraft skills would need brushing up after all this time. Maybe this holiday in Madeira was influencing her in a way she wouldn't have imagined while back home in the cottage she'd shared with John all those years.

So, was it time to leave her familiar surroundings? It would make sense to move at this point of her life, when she still had plenty of energy. But, as her son-in-law sometimes said to her, baby steps, Molly . . . baby steps. He had a lot of understanding of the human condition. She supposed that was why he'd chosen to become a social worker. It couldn't be that easy for Gavin and Tina to make ends meet, not with three young children. Her daughter didn't complain though, so they must be managing. Tom, on the other hand, commanded a good salary now as departmental head in a big comprehensive school. And Lucy worked three days a week in a hairdressing salon while the children's other grandma cared for Melissa.

By the time Molly arrived in the restaurant and joined the rest of the early birds at the breakfast buffet counter, she'd persuaded herself to stay in the moment. There'd be time enough to review her future after she got home. Except, of course, she had her caring commitment to think of. She couldn't just please herself and ignore what others might think or want.

'We must stop meeting like this.'

Molly glanced sideways to find Michael smiling at her. He'd piled cereal and slices of melon and peach into a bowl.

'I'm amazed I can even look at food after the dinner I put away last night,' he said.

'You need to sustain yourself for all that walking you'll be doing today. That's my excuse, anyway.'

Michael glanced towards the door and Molly spotted the same holidaymakers she and Kathy had shared a table with at the Botanical Gardens.

'Ah, sorry, but I need to confirm something with those two,' said Michael. 'I'll leave you to enjoy your breakfast. Have a good day, Molly.'

He set off across the room, leaving

Molly to make her choice from the appetising dishes set out. What more did she expect? He was at work. His job was to manage a group of clients whose various needs demanded priority. And to make matters worse, here was Kathy, surprisingly early for once, and probably about to tease Molly.

'I hope Michael didn't run away on my account,' said Kathy with a wink. 'Okay if I sit with you, or is he coming back?'

'More to the point, how did you get on last night? Wasn't the lipstick lady one of the group?'

Kathy chuckled. 'I shouldn't give people nicknames. She's good fun, actually. I think she's someone who can't resist flirting. And most of the waiters enjoy playing up to her, so she's having a lovely time.'

'Good for her,' said Molly.

'Um, are you all right?' Kathy peered at her.

'I'm fine, thank you. I'll go and sit by the window.'

Molly headed towards a table set for two. She hadn't meant to sound tetchy but all of a sudden there seemed to be too much going on in her life and far too many things to think about.

After Kathy arrived at the table with her yoghurt and fruit and their friendly waiter poured their coffee, Molly decided to confide in her companion. Kathy had also had to deal with the suddenly single predicament.

'I'm trying to work a few things out while I'm away from home, Kathy. Do you think that's sensible?'

Kathy looked sharply at Molly. 'You mean, looking at a situation from a distance instead of being right at the heart of it?'

'I suppose I do. Please don't feel you have to tell me anything confidential, but after . . . you know, after your marriage ended, were you forced to move house?'

Kathy stirred thick honey into her yoghurt. 'Yum. And yes, I was. My ex-husband couldn't cope with being a family man. I didn't want to be out socialising with him all the time. I knew we had to put the children first, but it was necessary to sell our house and find two smaller properties.'

'I expect that was a wrench?'

'Of course. But I managed to find somewhere not far from my parents, and that was a bonus because they were brilliant when it came to childcare. I didn't want to leave the town where I was brought up and of course I didn't want my daughters to have to change schools. They'd had enough upheaval.'

Molly nodded. 'You put your family first.'

'Or, you could say, I made the best of a bad situation. So, something positive came out of it.'

'My situation isn't a bad one, but I had a text from my daughter last night, inviting me to stay for Christmas. Maybe I'm wrong but I'm reading something into this.'

'Sounds to me as though she's very fond of you.'

'I see so little of her. You know, I'm wondering whether to put my cottage on the market when I get back.'

Kathy whistled. 'That's a big decision. I'd say, wait until you get home and are settled in again before you decide. Being here is living in a kind of dream world — marking time between life before and life after our holiday. If you stand in your own kitchen, look around and decide the time has come to move on, that's when you should talk to your family.'

Molly nodded. 'Thank you. I think that's wise advice.'

'And, Molly, please don't make such an important decision because you feel guilty over being unable to help your daughter. You have to consider your own needs, so if you're happy as you are, maybe you should wait a while before you review the situation.'

Molly stared at Kathy. 'You've been very helpful. Now, I'm going to make the most of being on holiday and fetch myself some ham and eggs before the hordes descend on the buffet! How about you? We'll have lots of walking today, don't forget.'

4

Plotting and Walking

Tina spooned scrambled egg into her younger son's mouth. 'There you go, Sam. Yummy!'

He waved a toast finger at her. She leaned forward and nipped off the end with her teeth. He pushed the remainder into his mouth and munched contentedly.

Tina grabbed the opportunity to examine the mail Gavin had left on the kitchen table before he'd driven Sophie and Jack to school. She recognised the handwriting on the cream envelope and what she read sent her to the kettle to make a strong cup of tea.

Fair View. Friday

My dear Tina and Gavin,
You know I'm one of those rare

folk who still enjoy writing letters, so here I am with some thoughts as well as a suggestion that I hope you'll approve of.

Firstly, your uncle and I have fallen in love with the look of Halliday House. It has sleeping accommodation for 16 people within six bedrooms. It's pet-friendly and hopefully no one will mind if we bring dear old Rosie, who's arguably better behaved than either of her owners! Anyway, if it's a problem, I can ask if our neighbours would like an extra Christmas guest. That hound of ours treats them like a second set of parents.

I'm sure everyone would enjoy having a heated indoor pool. There's also a games room, and I see the outdoor playground has a swing, so all we want is some kind weather so the children can play ball or Frisbee. I like the look of the kitchen — very spacious — important when we'll have several cooks. But this isn't the time to talk about who'll be doing what.

And you must be aware that Halliday House ticks all the boxes, as people say these days. I particularly like the idea of being able to walk into the nearby village and attend the Christmas morning church service.

Now for the nitty-gritty! A couple of months ago, Chris and I received a little windfall from one of his relations. It's not a life-changing sum of money, but very acceptable. We've already decided to give each of the children cash for their bank accounts, but Chris has come up with an idea and I fully agree with him. We'd like to pay for the house rental in full, whether it's for Halliday House or another one. We realise our first choice might be already taken, in which case we're happy for the rest of you to decide. If you don't have to consult us again, it'll save time.

We'll also bring some goodies plus, of course, stocking fillers for the littlies! I'm sure, further down the line, we'll all be allocated jobs. When

Molly rings me to report she's back, I'll be sure to say absolutely nothing about this. After all, it is a whole six months away, as I write. But preparations need to be made, so I'll stop rambling and look forward to hearing from you when you confirm that exciting reservation.

Much love and hugs to everyone,
Helen and Chris (and Rosie of course) xx

PS: We suggest you make the booking for seven nights, unless of course that proves impossible. People could choose to stay for just a few nights or for a whole week, which is what Chris and I would like to do. We walk in all weathers, and don't know the Cotswolds, so this seems like a golden opportunity to catch up with our nearest and dearest as well as get out from under their feet now and then!

PPS: Dave likes the idea, but it's probably early days for checking if his

*girlfriend would come too. I hope
that would be OK, if she's still
around by then!*

Tina looked up from the letter. Sam
was contentedly munching his egg and
toast, plastic spoon firmly grasped in
his pudgy little fist.

'Good boy, Sam,' said his mum. 'If
you only knew how generous Auntie
Helen and Uncle Chris are being. Wait
till I tell your daddy.'

She frowned. Should she text Gavin
and her brother? Everyone liked the
look of this Cotswolds property. Auntie
Helen was right when she said it ticked
all their boxes. But even though the sun
shone outside and the festive season
would normally be far from her
thoughts, others would also be looking
forward. Didn't brides and grooms
need to book their wedding venues
more than a year ahead?

That decided her. She sent a text to
her husband, knowing he'd be in a case
conference but would check his mobile

when he could. She decided not to interrupt her brother but sent a message to Lucy instead. If this happened to be a day when her sister-in-law worked at the salon, she'd be sure to have her phone handy, in case of something to do with little Melissa. Lucy would know when best to text Tom. Even if they didn't make the initial booking request until evening, at least they'd be one more step towards it.

Most importantly, Tina needed to respond to her aunt and uncle's amazingly generous offer. On a pristine sheet of proper writing paper. Written with a real pen. She'd need to fish around in one of the dresser drawers, but such a lovely gesture couldn't possibly be acknowledged by text or email.

She reached for the ever-handy damp flannel and wiped her little son's face and hands. 'Your nana would be stunned to know what was going on behind her back, Sam. But I haven't a clue what she needs to talk to me about. All I hope is that she hasn't made plans of her own for Christmas.'

She placed Sam on the floor near a stack of brightly coloured bricks. 'There you go, poppet. I'm just going to send a text to that nana of yours. She needs to know I mean business.'

* * *

Molly stood still and aimed her camera at the most beautiful waterfall she'd ever seen. Since the last one, of course. She'd been lucky enough to visit Niagara Falls with her late husband after he retired. These cascades and small lakes amongst the woodland didn't offer the same magnificence, but she loved strolling beside the levadas. The guide had given his tourist group hints about walking on the prescribed paths and keeping an eye on the person in front.

Kathy walked in front of Molly. She also carried a camera, and fortunately all the walkers seemed happy to stop when the next beautiful view appeared, taking photographs or drinking in the magical vista. When they saw the teahouse loom like a mirage in the desert, a little murmur of appreciation rippled along the line. No one wanted to miss out on this part of the tour, and Molly was amused to notice those who'd been lagging behind suddenly found that extra bit of energy needed to access the tea terrace.

'I wish my tiny patio at home had some of these fabulous plants growing on it.' Kathy looked around enviously.

'We do have some sub-tropical plants at home in Cornwall, but I can't compete with those giant tree ferns.'

'At least I've got a blue hydrangea in a tub and a couple of fuchsias.'

'Well that's brilliant. And they'll burgeon as time goes by. Baby steps, as my son-in-law would say. Baby steps, Kathy. It's quite crowded, isn't it? Shall we ask those two ladies over there if we may sit at their table?'

As she read the tempting choices on the menu, Molly wondered whether she really needed honey cake. Or orange cake? Or fresh scones with raspberry jam and cream, as Kathy suggested. The answer was no. But if she didn't eat something, she'd be ravenous by mid-afternoon.

Noticing Kathy checking her mobile, Molly remembered she'd switched hers off while walking the peaceful, sheltered trails. She discovered she had one message, not surprisingly from her daughter again.

Happy to talk but please note in your diary you're with us for Christmas, love Tina x

'Everything all right?' Kathy glanced at Molly as she poured two cups of tea.

'Fine, thanks. My daughter's made it plain I'm to spend Christmas with them.'

'You know you'll love it. Even if you decide to put your house on the market, it could take a while; and if it sells quickly, you'll be able to stay with them while you house-hunt. Sorted!'

Molly laughed. 'You're worse than

Tina. Did I say they live in west Wales?'

'I think so. Is it like Cornwall?'

Molly cut into her slice of luscious honey cake. 'In some ways, yes. Both have amazing coastlines and beauty spots, though you might find yourself driving a long way to go to the theatre or a big shopping centre. That wouldn't bother me though, and I like walking and being able to get to a beach like they can.'

'It sounds perfect.' Kathy buttered a second scone. 'I think you've almost made up your mind, but don't forget what I said.'

'No, I won't forget, my dear. But I'm more and more convinced I need to put my family first.'

'They'll be lucky to have you.'

'If I do make this move, I'm determined not to live in their pockets. I wouldn't just turn up on the doorstep.'

'I can't imagine you ever doing that. How about if the boot was on the other foot? If your daughter arrived out of the blue and asked if you could take the children for a few hours?'

Molly considered. 'If it was an emergency, of course I'd drop everything. But I see where you're coming from. I'd expect Tina to respect my privacy as I'd respect hers.'

'That sounds like an ideal arrangement.'

Molly glanced upwards. 'It's turning very misty, don't you think?'

'And a bit chilly.' Kathy reached into her bag and pulled out a cardigan. 'Is this normal, I wonder?'

'We're quite high here, don't forget. As we descend again, it'll probably be warmer.'

'Looks like our guide's going to gather his flock.'

'Don't rush,' said Molly. 'He seems to be giving everyone a ten-minute warning.'

'Well, let's hope we all get in and out of the washrooms.'

Fortunately everyone gained gold stars for good behaviour, but on the way back

Molly felt as if the dank mist was chilling her right through to her bones. The trees formed eerie shapes, and once or twice people couldn't resist stopping to take a quirky, creepy photograph. They reached the pick-up point to find their coach waiting.

'I wouldn't have missed that for worlds,' said Kathy once they boarded and set off for Funchal. 'In spite of that spooky mist.'

'I could do without the air-conditioning,' said Molly. 'I might take a swim when we get back. The pool's going to feel like a warm bath after that foggy stuff. But I agree, it was a wonderful experience.'

'Maybe a quiet day would be a good idea tomorrow. I haven't booked up for anything. How about you?'

'I wondered about the wine lodge tours. If you fancy that tomorrow, I don't mind going down early to book places.'

'Or we could ask Michael?'

'Um, yes, we could,' said Molly.

'I'm not sure I want to sample the wines, but I'm happy to go along and learn something new.'

'Okay, we'll speak to Michael later.'

'Or you can,' said Kathy with a wink. 'Tell you what. Unbelievable as it may seem, I'm beginning to feel peckish again.'

★   ★   ★

'I could eat a horse,' said Gavin as he came through the door.

'Silly Daddy,' said his daughter.

'Or maybe I could eat a Sophie. Or a Jack. Or a baby Sam. Grrrr . . . '

The two elder children lunged at their dad, screeching with delight, and the three collapsed in giggles on the hall floor, limbs waving around like bendy dolls.

'I'm afraid you'll have to make do with pasta and homemade sauce tonight, sir.'

Gavin remained flat on the floor. Sophie occupied his stomach. Jack sat on his feet. 'I've been grounded,' he said.

'I expect Daddy would like a nice cuppa,' said Tina, plonking Sam on his father's chest. 'I'll put the kettle on and we can compare notes.'

'Any chance of cake?' Gavin asked hopefully.

'We saved you some flapjack, Daddy,' said Sophie.

'Ace.'

Tina made tea, listening to happy sounds that she thought might be racing cars vroom vrooming, or maybe horses neighing, knowing how Sophie fell in love with every pony she came across, whether in a field or a picture in a book.

While the elder two watched a DVD and Gavin munched homemade flapjack and took swallows of tea while playing with Sam, Tina asked if there'd been any progress regarding their big project.

'We should really have a code word,' said Gavin. 'Like in the war.'

'None of us were alive in World War Two, fortunately,' said Tina.

'But we've watched the movies. I'll have a think. What was your question again?'

'Gavin!'

'Okay, okay — only teasing. Your brother rang me at lunchtime. Well, his lunchtime, anyway. I was in the car but I pulled over and spoke to him. He said he'd make the booking via the website. Oh, and he said he and Lucy are very touched by Helen and Chris's offer.'

'It's fabulous, isn't it? But have you heard anything since?'

'He's going to Skype us tonight. By which time he should have an answer.'

All the children were in bed by the time the couples made contact.

'Would you believe the family that booked Halliday House last year made an immediate booking for this year?'

'Oh, no,' said Tina. She bit her lip, trying not to feel too disappointed. 'So, have you made a booking for our second choice?'

'No.' Tom grinned. 'That would be pointless.'

Gavin and Tina looked at one another.

'Don't tell me that's taken as well!'

'I don't know.' He paused. 'But here's the amazing thing. The owner of Halliday House rang us not long ago to say the original booking had been cancelled. Apparently one of the family members has taken a job in Florida and the rest of the clan have decided to fly out there for Christmas.'

'So, we can have the house?' Gavin grabbed his wife's hand.

'We can indeed,' said Tom. 'I'm sorry we took a while contacting you but hopefully the good news will make up for that.'

'It's wonderful. Thanks, Tom,' said Tina. 'I've been in touch with Mum, though only by text. All I said was that we'd like her to spend Christmas with us this year, but I received a strange reply. She said we needed to talk.'

'That doesn't sound like her. Maybe

you happened to catch her at a bad time.'

'That's what I think,' said Gavin. 'Her mind's far from being on Christmas but logically, having you three with her last year, you'd think she'd be pleased to spend the next one with us.'

'Well, keep us posted.' Tom frowned. 'She couldn't possibly have decided to book another foreign holiday for December, could she? That would ruin everything.'

5

A Knight in Shining Armour

After returning to her hotel room, Molly changed into her swimsuit, put on casual trousers and a sweatshirt, and pushed her feet into flip-flops. There were changing rooms at the poolside, so she quickly stashed her things in a locker and dropped her towel on a lounger at the shallow end. Most people hadn't returned from their excursions but the female lifeguard on duty gave her a wave as she supervised some children. Molly wasn't a strong swimmer but loved trying to beat her own record of lengths achieved each time she used a pool. The hotel one was a decent size but not daunting like the Olympic-size one she'd used in Plymouth a while back, when staying with a friend.

She slipped into the warm water and took a couple of steps before launching herself into a gentle breaststroke that her children used to tease her about, telling her she swam as though trying to protect her hairstyle. The thought amused her as she headed down the pool, deciding to complete four lengths before going back to her room for a shower and rest.

When she tried to clamber up the steps to leave the water, for some reason one foot slipped and she fell forward, banging her head on the poolside. Molly slid back into the water and sank beneath the surface.

Michael, making his way down the path towards the lounging area, noticed the lifeguard leap into action, so sprinted along the grassy strip in front of the line of deckchairs and loungers. He beat the young Portuguese employee to it, arriving just in time to see a head disappear beneath the surface of the water.

He jumped straight in, hauled the inert body upwards and draped her on the tiled poolside, where the young lifeguard swiftly put Molly into the recovery position. Michael, his dark green polo shirt and cream linen trousers dripping wet, climbed out of the pool and bent over the unconscious woman. He gasped as he saw who he'd rescued.

'She's in my group. Is she all right?'

The lifeguard's face remained impassive. 'She's breathing fine, but we need to get her to hospital in case she's concussed. Will you ring, please, Michael?'

Michael pulled out his mobile phone, praying it still worked, and made a call. He knew all the front-of-house hotel staff pretty well and was aware Molly was in good hands. But his heart hammered as he waited for his call to be answered. He had a basic knowledge of the Portuguese language, but the islanders' accent often made it difficult for him to understand them, so he stuck to English.

'They're sending an ambulance,' he said.

The lifeguard looked up at him. 'What, please, is her name?'

'Mrs Reid — Molly.'

'Okay, Molly. Can you hear me?'

Michael hurried over to the chairs and picked up a towel. 'I can't bear to see her lying there without protection, even on a sunny afternoon,' he said, spreading the towel over the inert form.

'I think she say something,' said the lifeguard.

Michael crouched beside Molly. 'Can you hear us, Molly? It's Michael.'

The lifeguard gently massaged Molly's hands and arms. She opened her eyes.

'Please not to move,' said the lifeguard.

'Oh, my dear, you've given us such a shock,' said Michael. 'Can you speak to us? Don't nod your head.'

Molly's blurred vision cleared enough to recognise the tour guide, his eyes not crinkling with amusement but filled with concern as he looked down at her.

'I can hear you. Oh, dear, I'm so sorry to be such a nuisance.'

Michael smiled. 'You can't imagine how relieved I am to hear you speaking. Just keep nice and still, now. We've sent for assistance and we don't want to move you as long as you can hang in there.'

'I'm not going anywhere, unless it's back to my room.'

The lifeguard patted Molly's hand. 'Is best you go to hospital for examination.'

Molly closed her eyes again. Suddenly she felt very, very tired.

★ ★ ★

'Have you heard anything more from your mother?' Gavin appeared in the utility room doorway.

Tina closed the door of the washing machine and set the cycle in motion. 'Nope. Not since her last text. She must be all right though, else someone would have been in touch, don't you think?'

'It's a reputable tour company with a guide accompanying them. She's obviously having a great time.' Gavin moved to let his wife through to the kitchen.

'Molly doesn't do Facebook, so we'll have to wait 'til she gets back. Mind you, there's so much you can look up on line, I'll probably feel I know some of the places she'll have visited.'

'They had those dreadful floods out there a few years back. It must have been frightening, especially as the climate's normally so temperate.'

'Mum did her research months and months ago, when she decided to book a holiday.'

'When's she due back?'

'This Saturday. I'll give her a ring Sunday and see if she's in a talking mood.'

'While crossing your fingers and hoping she hasn't booked for turkey and tinsel in Lapland or maybe even Barbados?'

'You have to be joking!'

'Time will tell,' said Gavin. 'I think I hear Sam. I'll get him up.'

'And I'll make us cheese on toast.'

'Sounds good. By the way, Chris emailed to say they'd paid the deposit on our house and received confirmation. We can sit back and forget it until nearer the time.'

'Great. Let's hope Mum was playing hard to get and that we won't all find ourselves in the Cotswolds without her.'

Gavin rolled his eyes and headed for the baby's room.

Tina collected sliced bread and cheese from the fridge. She switched on the grill and wondered what her mother was doing at that moment. Was she sipping a cool drink while relaxing beside the hotel pool? Or was she sitting on a coach, gazing at spectacular scenery and wondering what she'd be having for lunch?

She stopped slicing cheese as another scenario occurred to her. What if her mum was sitting beside some silver-haired gentleman while he poured out his heart? She knew she shouldn't worry, but was this how Molly had felt when Tina had first gone on a date with a boy in the same year at school? Worried how her daughter might be perceived by the opposite sex?

But this was different. Her mother surely wasn't looking for romance? Gavin would tell her not to be silly; remind her again that her mother needed to move on. But that little feeling of apprehension wouldn't budge and she decided Sunday couldn't come fast enough. But she wouldn't interrogate her mum. Just maybe enquire, in a casual kind of way, of course, whether Molly had put a line in her diary, through the week commencing 23rd December.

* * *

Michael stuck his head round the doorway of the ward where Molly was sitting up in bed. He walked slowly towards her, clutching a large plastic carrier bag. She noticed the relieved smile on his face.

'This is all very silly. I can't apologise enough for being so careless and causing such trouble.'

'Well, it's good to see you sitting up and doubtless putting the world to rights.' He pulled up a chair.

'Thank goodness I made sure to take out decent travel insurance.'

'As they say, one never knows. But the main thing is, you didn't injure yourself badly. Have they said when you can leave hospital?'

'Tomorrow morning, all being well, but I have to wait until the consultant does his rounds.'

Michael took out his diary. 'I think that's the full-day excursion to the side of the island we haven't yet visited — yes, it is. I'm sorry I can't come and collect you, Molly. But I can arrange for one of the hotel staff to book a taxi and take you back. I'll ask them to liaise with the hospital and you won't need to do a thing. Kathy has packed a few things for you, as you went in, um, you know . . . ' He placed the bag on her bed.

'Not really dressed for polite company, was I? I hadn't really thought about it. I'm so pleased not to have broken any bones.' She lifted up the bag, peered inside and riffled around. 'Oh, she's a star. Someone obviously sorted out my locker. All I want is to get back to the tour and enjoy my last couple of days in Madeira.'

'Of course. I was wondering, would you like me to ring your daughter or your son? As you know, I have both their telephone numbers in my file.'

'I really don't want to worry them, Michael. But thanks for the thought. My mobile phone's still in my room, I imagine. I can contact them tomorrow if necessary.' She grinned. 'There'll probably be a couple of messages from Tina, though why the heck she's so keen on planning Christmas when it's only June, I have no idea.'

'But you're very lucky that your family are so keen to book you, don't you think?' He sounded wistful.

Molly bit her lip. 'I'm sorry if put my foot in it. I didn't mean to sound flippant. To be honest, I'm feeling a little demoralised by what happened.'

'That's understandable, given you've had a nasty experience. Losing consciousness is a shock to the system. Especially when you had to come round and realise you were far from home. Then you're carted off to a strange hospital. I think you're coping brilliantly.'

'Everyone's been very kind, I know. But this is your working day — having to visit me is stopping you from carrying out your normal duties.'

'Spending time with you is a pleasure, Molly. But I do have to go now, because I'm speaking at a tourism association dinner this evening.'

'Are you looking forward to it?'

'Not really! I've spoken at similar functions, so I know what to expect. I'm always a little nervous before these things, though. I much prefer the cut and thrust of guiding my groups around.'

'Well I'd award you five stars, that's for sure.'

He shot her his crinkly-eyed smile. 'Promise you won't get into trouble if I leave you now?'

'I promise.' She smiled up at him.

And when he'd gone, she was left with a warm feeling such as she hadn't experienced since being widowed. Michael had said all the right things, but that was only to be expected, given the qualifications he needed in order to do his job properly. She happened to be a member of his current group and after he saw them all safely on to their flight at the weekend, he'd be welcoming another bunch of eager tourists. He might remember her as the woman who narrowly escaped a calamity; but apart from the odd casual conversation over the last week, that was all.

What more could she expect?

★   ★   ★

When Molly was transported by wheelchair to the hospital's main entrance, she saw a familiar face.

'Kathy! I'm so pleased to see you.' Molly remembered her manners and smiled at the uniformed hotel receptionist standing beside her travel companion. 'It's Joana, isn't it? Thank you for coming to fetch me.'

'We're pleased you are able to complete your holiday, Mrs Reid.'

'I can't tell you how relieved I am to see you, Molly. You gave us all such a fright.' Kathy turned to the orderly who'd brought Molly from the ward. 'My friend can get into the taxi now?'

The man nodded. 'Formalities finish. Goodbye, Mrs Reid.'

'Goodbye. You've all been very kind but I'll try not to come back.'

On the way, Molly apologised to Kathy for interrupting her holiday.

'Don't be silly. We'd planned a quiet day anyway. Maybe we should give the wine tasting a miss, though.'

'I expect you're right.'

'You need to take things easy. Did the hospital issue any instructions?'

'Only to take things easy. Oh, and on

no account to go swimming.'

'I almost forgot.' Kathy scrabbled in her handbag and produced a phone. 'Joana let me into your room so I could collect some clothes for you and I noticed your mobile on the bedside cabinet.'

'That was a kind thought. I left it switched off, so let's just have a look.' She pressed the button and waited. 'No, there are no urgent messages awaiting my attention, thank goodness.'

'Will you tell your family about what happened?'

'Not until after I get back. Then my daughter can scold me to her heart's content without having to worry about me travelling back to Cornwall.'

'There's something happening after dinner this evening that might interest you,' Joana chimed in. 'Michael's giving a talk about his experiences as a tour guide. He says it's a shorter, funnier version of the formal talk he had to give last night.'

'There,' said Kathy. 'A chance to

learn all about your knight in shining armour, Molly!'

'I'll see how I feel.'

'Would you like me to stay with you this afternoon?'

Molly considered. 'I don't want to spoil your fun, but though I hate to admit it, I feel a wee bit shaky.'

'The hotel will be quiet at that time, Mrs Reid,' said Joana. 'If you choose a sun lounger in the shade, you can put your feet up. I can tell the team to keep an eye open for you.'

Molly turned to Kathy. 'There you are. I shall have a babysitter and won't be shut in my room, nice though it is with that little balcony. You should go out somewhere, Kathy. Make the most of it.'

★　★　★

Later, from her seat on the terrace, Molly gazed at the hotel gardens. She was going to miss all these beautiful plants but she knew, once she set eyes on her own little patch, her fingers would itch to get out there weeding, dead-heading and inspecting the greenhouse which her neighbour was tending during her absence.

She looked up and smiled at sight of a waiter bringing her a tall drink. Ice cubes clinked as he placed the glass on a paper cocktail mat on the table beside her.

'That looks delicious,' she said. 'Sadly, I didn't order it.'

The waiter smiled back at her. 'It is from your tour manager, Mr Michael.'

'Goodness. I didn't know he was here.'

'I took the liberty of ordering drinks for you and me.' Michael walked towards her, glass in hand. 'These mocktails are, of course, entirely non-alcoholic. May I join you?'

She moved her magazine from the table. 'Please do. How's your day going so far?'

'Busy.' He raised his glass to her. 'Cheers. We linked up with another tour operator, so we filled one full-size coach. Shall we say it was a little stressful, counting my chicks plus the extra ones each time we boarded after a stop, but everyone was very well-behaved.'

'It must be difficult when you realise someone's missing. Does that happen much?'

His eyes twinkled. 'Ah, I shall be talking about that sort of thing this evening. Do you think you might feel like attending?'

'I do hope so. I imagine some of your experiences are very amusing?'

'You could say that, but I'm sure anyone who works with people must have lots of comical experiences along the way.'

'As well as the not-so-funny goings-on like my head-banging demonstration in the pool.'

'Molly, you mustn't beat yourself up about that.'

She laughed. 'No pun intended!'

'Come on, we're all very thankful you're safely back with us. At dinner last night, I had no end of enquiries about your welfare.'

She shifted in her chair. 'Goodness. People are very kind, aren't they? The staff here couldn't have been more considerate.'

'Fortunately most are, in my opinion. We won't talk about the exceptions — after all, this is your holiday.'

'Holidays are a chance to count our blessings, I always think. I've been on trips abroad where I've looked through the window of our comfortable air-conditioned coach, and caught my breath at some of the sights in the poverty-stricken village we were passing through.'

'I have to harden my heart to beggars, especially children, though that's difficult to do.'

'I bet you find it impossible not to hand over a few coins to youngsters,' said Molly.

'Yes, you're absolutely right. In some places the local economy would fall flat on its face if people like us didn't take our holidays there.'

'So, after you wave us through the

departure gate on Saturday, do you have another group arriving?'

'I do indeed. Another 32 people; but after that, I have a few days off. I shall be going home to Wales.'

'I didn't know you lived in Wales. My daughter and family are in Pembrokeshire.'

'I live near Cardiff,' he said. 'But I know Pembrokeshire well.' He looked at his watch. 'I must make a move. One of the hotels we use has had a change of management and I need to go along and chat to a few people. As you can imagine, it's important to check that standards remain high.'

'So, inspections are among your duties? It must be hectic for you, this time of year.'

'My employer is also an old friend, so I'm lucky that he trusts me to carry out a, shall we say, more varied role than merely a tour guide. It's more interesting that way — but I mustn't talk shop, must I?'

While he finished his drink, Molly

wondered if he had anyone back in Wales eagerly awaiting his return. If so, she envied them. But she kept her thoughts to herself.

* * *

There were around twenty guests waiting to hear Michael recount his tour experiences when Kathy and Molly walked into the small conference room.

'I keep forgetting to ask the poor man whether his clothes were ruined when he jumped in the pool to rescue me,' Molly murmured as they took their seats.

'Hopefully not. But he'll be able to claim on his expenses, surely.' Kathy giggled. 'Is he married? Do you think he'll tell his wife about diving in to save a damsel in distress?'

'A somewhat mature but very grateful damsel,' said Molly. 'Or damson, according to my little Sophie.'

'That's cute,' said Kathy. 'You're

going to have to visit them soon, aren't you? I can tell by the look in your eye when you mention your grandchildren, how much you miss them.'

'Here's our speaker.' Molly was glad to change the subject. She was also fearful of nodding off during Michael's talk. Not that she thought he'd bore them all to tears; far from it. She still felt not quite herself — as if she was watching proceedings from a different angle. Maybe she really should go for a check-up after her return, as the consultant had recommended. He'd reassured her there was nothing worrying happening inside her brain. She hadn't told him her own thoughts could be worrying enough without unwelcome intrusions like bumps on the head.

Luckily, Molly had no trouble with focusing on Michael's account of living life out of a suitcase. He had an easy way of putting facts over and often invited people in the audience to say whether they'd experienced whatever incident he was relating.

'So far,' he said as he neared the end of his talk, 'I've not had to drive off without the full complement of passengers on board.'

'Have you ever had to send out a search party?' Molly summoned the courage to ask.

Michael smiled at her. 'Yes, I have. I was working as a tour guide in Canada and one of the people in my charge became disorientated and wandered down the wrong road. Sat on a bench and dropped off to sleep.'

'Whatever did you do?' the lipstick lady asked.

'I asked our driver and a couple of tour members who I knew were ex-forces to spread out and find the gentleman. One of them came upon him still slumbering, gently woke him, and marched him straight back.'

'Sounds like this happened before the days mobile phones became so popular,' someone in the front row said.

'Yes. It was in the 1990s; I seem to

remember people had them more for work reasons, and the company I worked for hadn't got around to supplying them. Now, of course, I have all your phone numbers saved while you're in my group. Even now, though, I find the occasional person who dislikes the idea of owning a mobile.'

He looked around. 'I'm sure you've put up with me droning on long enough. The night is young, so go for a stroll, enjoy something to drink on the terrace. And those of you with me tomorrow, I shall see you in reception at eight o'clock.'

As everyone dispersed, Molly stayed sitting down, with Kathy beside her.

Michael came and sat beside Kathy. 'I know you're both booked on tomorrow's tour. Are you quite certain you feel up to it, Molly? I can arrange for a reimbursement, so please don't feel you have to join us. Though I hope you do.'

'I hate the thought of missing out.' Molly moved her head gently from side

6

Codename Mistletoe

'Mum's home. She rang the landline.' Tina walked across the back lawn. 'I see you're giving Daddy a hand, Sam.'

Gavin dumped another load of grass cuttings on the heap. 'I don't know about that, but he's having a great time. So she's all right?'

'Yep. It was just a quick call to say she'd arrived safe and sound and will ring tomorrow morning. She seems to have enjoyed herself. Wishes, of course, that she and Dad had made the trip while they still could.'

'That's understandable. So, tact and diplomacy tomorrow, I suppose.'

'I hope she'll bring the subject up. If not, it might seem a bit pushy talking about Codename Mistletoe when she's hardly put her holiday clothes through the washing machine.'

Gavin scooped up Sam from the grass pile. Tina held out her arms. 'Give him to me, love. I'll put him in the pushchair and take the three of them to the swings while you finish mowing. They can all go in the bath before tea then.'

'I'll walk along to meet you in a bit. There's not much left to do.'

Tina set off with the three children, Sophie skipping in front and Jack gripping one of the pushchair handles while keeping an eye open for cats, his current passion. Tina realised how lucky she was having Gavin, who enjoyed being a dad. He was incredibly untidy around the house, but she could put up with mysterious piles of paperwork and having to seek out missing socks and even empty lunchboxes as long as he continued giving her the kind of help she appreciated.

With a guilty pang, she thought how many hours of childcare her brother and sister-in-law received from Lucy's mother. On the rare occasions Tina's mum visited, she was brilliant with the children. But Sam and probably Jack wouldn't recognise Molly if she appeared in the playground now. Even Sophie would put on her shy act and hide while she got used to this unfamiliar grandma being around. The two younger ones probably connected her only with Skype, like a character from one of the CBeebies programmes they so enjoyed.

While Sophie happily ran off to play on the slide, having found a friend from her class at school, Tina gave Jack a push or two to start him swinging. She forestalled any indignant yells from Sam by placing her younger son in one of the baby seats and gently rocking him backwards and forwards while Jack showed off by flexing his legs to make himself fly higher.

She watched an elderly couple, presumably with their grandchildren. Gran was shadowing an active toddler while Granddad hung on to a pushchair, looking as if he wished he could be at home, tending his roses. But the children's mum was probably making use of every precious minute of this time. Unless, of course (Tina smiled to herself), she was at home with a new baby.

That period of time after Sam was born, when Molly came to stay after Gavin's paternity leave ended, still made her feel grateful. Her mum had done the minimum of housework but cooked delicious meals and even held baking sessions with Sophie and a slightly worried-looking Jack. Those days would never be forgotten. Now, Tina resolved to invite her mum to come and stay whenever she felt inclined. But straightaway, she remembered Molly's caring role. She couldn't be so arrogant as to ask her mother to give up something she obviously enjoyed.

Gavin appeared in the gateway and waved before strolling over to Sophie to give her a cuddle. Then he headed towards his wife and sons. 'Guess what?' His eyes sparkled with merriment.

'My poor brain won't allow me to make guesses,' said Tina. 'Take pity on me, Gav.'

'Molly rang.'

'Again? What's happened?'

'She's fine. She'll ring again tomorrow as planned, but she's had some unexpected news which means she's free to come and stay with us. She suggests the school holidays, because that's when you've got the three scamps all at home, but she says we're to discuss it and sort out a date.'

'This must be something to do with the neighbour she helps look after. Oh dear, I wonder if the worst has happened.'

'Your mum didn't say, but she sounded relieved. So I wouldn't think it's what you're suggesting.'

'Nor me. I get the impression Mum's very fond of the old lady, and she'd be sad if anything happened to her.'

'What we do know is that caring has been a tie for Molly. Maybe she needs some breathing space.'

'She won't get much chance to draw breath when she's with us.' Tina watched Sophie solemnly helping a smaller child off the slide. 'It's lovely that Mum's first thought seems to have been about coming to stay with us, don't you think?'

'I knew you'd be pleased. We might even get a night or two out!'

'How about a date?'

'Sounds good. As long as I don't have to wear a tie.'

'No, Gav!' Tina giggled. 'I meant when should we suggest Mum comes to stay?'

7

Home Alone

Molly poured herself a glass of red wine, telling herself that after the news she'd just received, she deserved a little boost.

After ringing her daughter, she'd picked up a small scattering of mail from the doormat. She'd found a colourful post-card from a friend holidaying in Benidorm, and a handwritten letter among the leaf-lets and boring brown envelopes. The news the letter contained had stolen her breath. Its contents were all the more poignant, as she'd been considering whether or not to pop round and say hello to the elderly lady whose needs she looked after.

Dear Molly,
*   First of all, I hope you enjoyed your well-deserved holiday in Madeira.*

I know the climate is said to be idyllic and in the brochure you showed me, your hotel looked superb. I expect you enjoyed having a swimming pool handy!

I'm afraid I have some news to break to you. For a while now, I've been considering my mother's future. I'm sorry to say she had a little fall while you were away and having talked over the matter with her GP and with my husband, we've decided residential care is the best option.

So, while you've been on holiday, a lot has been going on and I apologise if you feel sidelined in any way. Please be assured that we have always found your care and consideration beyond reproach. Mum has become very fond of you and I know she'll miss you. But you cannot offer 24-hour care, and while we'd much prefer to have three Mollies looking after Mum in her own home, this isn't possible.

So my mother is staying with us temporarily, and we've located a suitable residential home only ten miles away. I'll send you the contact details as soon as everything's confirmed.

You'll find your bank account credited with an appropriate amount. If you've left any personal belongings at my mother's and would like to collect them, I shall be back next week. Please ring me so we can arrange a convenient time to meet at the bungalow. We're planning to put it on the market very soon.

Thanks again, Molly. God bless.
Margaret Mason

As soon as Molly had absorbed the information, she picked up the phone once again in what she supposed was a knee-jerk reaction to the abrupt change to her everyday life. Gavin had sounded cheerful as usual, and she'd smiled to hear his shout of *Yippee* when she asked whether she might come for a visit.

She sat staring into space. It didn't even matter that her suitcase remained unpacked. Nor that her fridge contained only the minimum and she required a few fresh food items to see her through the weekend. Molly knew she'd find something in the freezer ready to pop into the microwave that evening. Kathy's advice about taking great care over her future plans suddenly seemed to stand out in capital letters. The possibility of moving house became more attractive, the more she thought about it. She wasn't that ancient, for goodness' sake! Surely she'd make new friends if she moved to Wales. And Gavin would know all about volunteering opportunities.

Molly smiled as she imagined how her daughter would have reacted to the news of her mother coming to stay. Tina never moaned about Tom and Lucy being lucky to have a grandma living so close. Tina and Gavin's friends all had young families of their own, but with Molly staying they'd have a chance to go out as a couple whenever they wished. Even the most dedicated dads and mums valued an occasional break from little people.

But she'd need another week at home. Tomorrow morning she'd arrange to visit the bungalow, as recommended in the letter she'd received. There were a few personal items placed neatly in the spare-room wardrobe. She'd also lent the old lady some DVDs and books, the return of which would be appreciated. As for Molly's garden, there'd be plenty to keep her occupied. She needed to give it a tidy-up, though she felt the cottage, thanks to years of loving care, hardly needed much more than a lick of paint here and there.

Once she'd got things shipshape, to use her late husband's favourite expression, she could contact a couple of estate agencies and request a valuation. The thought sent a shiver down her spine, but an excited kind of shiver. Armed with up-to-date information, she could visit Tina and the family and discuss her decision with them.

But Molly knew she'd be very surprised indeed if her daughter and son-in-law didn't jump at the idea. And maybe she'd find out what was so urgent about booking her to stay over Christmas. She might even be living in Wales by then. If so, who knew what her future holiday plans might be.

★ ★ ★

On the appointed day, when her doorbell rang at exactly ten o'clock, Molly closed her eyes briefly, took a deep breath and went to let the first estate agent in.

Walking around the house that had been her home for more than twenty years, Molly realised how lucky she was. In some rooms where she'd feared the décor might be a little old-fashioned, the woman making the valuation declared that traditional was positive and the paintwork Molly privately thought of as maybe a little bland, became neutral.

The amount the estate agent figured the property should fetch in current market conditions made Molly blink.

Of course she'd become aware of rising prices over the decades, but having checked out the cost of houses in Tina and Gavin's region of Wales, she felt a frisson of excitement as she realised she should be able to buy a property with three bedrooms, which meant she could put up her son's family with ease. How about that for a Christmas suggestion?

But often houses didn't attract a buyer at once. It was all a bit of a lottery. So Molly decided to keep these private thoughts to herself and stick to her plan. By the time she left for Wales she'd have two valuations, and all she required was confirmation from Tina and Gavin that they'd be happy to have her living if not in the same road, maybe a few miles away.

On her own again, she decided to put in a couple of hours on the garden before taking a long, leisurely lunch break. She'd barely shaken off her Wellington boots when she heard her telephone ringing and picked up the kitchen extension, hands still grubby from her efforts.

'Molly? This is Michael Todd here. I'm ringing to see how you are.'

'I'm fine, thanks. But surely you're not ringing from Madeira?'

She heard him chuckle. 'I've been pulled out of Funchal. A new tour guide has replaced me for the time being. I'm back in London because someone went sick and I'm taking over a Canada tour.'

'Oh, lucky you. I know you've worked there before.'

'I'm looking forward to it, yes. So you're feeling back to normal?'

'Yes thank you, and keeping busy. My life has changed in different ways since my holiday.'

'Really? I hope you'll tell me all about it soon. You will keep in touch, Molly? You have my business card?'

'I do. I could email you if you like.'

'I'd like that very much. I must get myself to Heathrow now, but I suddenly thought of you and decided to pick up the phone.'

She blinked hard. 'I'm pleased you

did. I'll update you with my news soon, then.'

'I know you said you couldn't foresee a trip to Wales for the time being, but if you do happen to get there, please let me know. It would be really good to see you again. We could have a bit of lunch, maybe?' He sounded almost shy.

'When are you due back?'

'I should be back in Wales — let's say in fifteen days from now.'

'Right. Well, *bon voyage*.'

'Thanks, Molly. Take care.'

She put the phone down, then covered her mouth with her mud-stained fingers to hide the round O of surprise. Her heart was pitter-pattering with pleasure. This kind, busy man had taken time to contact her and ask how she was doing. Should she conclude this was part of his role, following up an unfortunate incident on behalf of the tour company as a gesture of goodwill? Slipping on the hotel pool's steps had been entirely her fault. She'd gone up and down them a couple of times before that last occasion.

But, to ring someone who'd been part of his tour group and suggest meeting for lunch was surely not included in his job description? She smiled and headed back to the garden. Michael would receive quite a surprise when he read the email she planned to send. And he wouldn't be the only one who'd be taken aback. She couldn't wait to break the news of her decision to Tina and Gavin.

8

Nothing Beats a Proper Hug

Tina met her mother at the nearest main line railway station. Having left plenty of time to make the 45-minute drive, she'd been delayed firstly by road works, then by a car transporter causing a tailback on a winding road where patience was the only way to deal with the inevitable slow progress.

As she hurried towards the station, she saw her mother come through the entrance.

'Mum!' Tina sprinted towards her.

Molly held out her arms. 'It's so wonderful to see you, my lovely.'

'And you.' Tina hugged her mother back. 'You look so well. That tan suits you.'

'I'm outdoors whenever I can be, these days.'

'Your holiday must have something to do with it, surely?' Tina took her mother's red wheelie case and started trundling it to the car park.

'Oh yes, Madeira was everything I hoped it would be.'

'So, no hitches? Travel arrangements all smooth? I wondered about you walking along those levada thingies, but you obviously didn't come to any harm.'

Molly hesitated. 'I won't bang on about it all, though I do have some lovely photographs. Towards the end of my stay, I had a little mishap.'

Tina zapped her key and opened the boot. 'Nothing too awful, I hope.'

'I slipped, climbing out of the swimming pool one afternoon, and, erm, ended up having a night in hospital. Only for observation,' she said hurriedly.

'Mum! Why on earth didn't you let us know?' Tina opened the car door for Molly.

'Because there was nothing you could do and I didn't want to worry you. Now I'm here and you can see I'm perfectly all right.' She settled into the front seat.

Tina got behind the wheel. 'So have you had a medical check since returning home?'

'The consultant at the hospital in Funchal recommended I do that, so of course I booked an appointment. I'm pleased to say my GP could find nothing to be concerned about.'

Tina started the engine. 'What a relief. Oh, Mum, poor you. All on your own in a strange place.'

'They were very kind to me. And Michael, our tour guide, couldn't have been more helpful.' She cleared her throat as Tina put the car in reverse gear. 'In fact, he happened to be nearby when I slipped — though he didn't realise it was me at that point — and he jumped straight into the shallow end and helped the lifeguard ease me out of the water.'

'So he was already in his swimsuit?'

'Sadly not. He was in his everyday clothes.'

'Poor man. Now that's what I call

customer service! Seriously though, Mum, you could've hurt yourself badly.'

'Well I didn't, and it was my own silly fault, Tina. No way did I even consider blaming the hotel. I think I must have turned my foot on the top rung, so I lost my balance and managed to bump my head as I fell sideways into the water.'

'You mustn't try to do too much while you're here. The children can't wait to see you in real life, as Sophie calls it, but I'll make sure they don't tire you out. Gavin's giving them tea and you'll see them before their bedtime.'

'Perfect.' Molly sighed. 'I've brought you each a little gift from Madeira.'

'How lovely. Jack and Sophie will be over the moon.'

'And after the little ones are in bed, I'd like to run something past you and Gavin.'

'Is this to do with your carer job ending? Are you considering something else? Surely you don't need to go out to work, Mum?'

'I'm lucky that I don't, but caring for my nearby neighbour came about gradually. In a strange kind of way, having been on holiday on my own, so to speak, and coming home to find I've lost that job, I realise something else might be around the corner. Let's say it's a combination of things triggering my new way of thinking.'

'Sounds intriguing,' said Tina.

'Anyway, thank goodness we've kept in touch by Skype,' said Molly. 'Otherwise I'd probably be amazed at how much the children have grown.'

'It's much nicer for you to see them in the flesh though, Mum.'

'Of course! Nothing beats a proper hug.'

Molly steered the conversation back to Madeira and its sub-tropical plants and foliage. She mentioned Kathy and said they'd got on well despite the age difference.

'What about your superhero tour guide? Was he as good at his job as he was at jumping fully clothed into a pool?'

'Michael's a charming man. He went out of his way to make sure everyone enjoyed their holiday.'

Tina pulled up at a road junction. Molly glanced around at the fields, at the sheep grazing, and at a roadside inn where mums and dads sat outside enjoying drinks in the early evening sunshine while their children frolicked on a bouncy castle.

'It's lovely here, isn't it? Do you get many folk buying houses for retirement?'

'I'm not sure,' said Tina, turning right. 'Maybe they do nearer the coast. It seems quite a good mix of age groups in our neck of the woods.' She changed gear. 'Why are you interested, Mother, dear? It's lovely in Cornwall as well, isn't it?'

Molly chuckled. 'Of course. I'm keeping my options open, but I think we should wait to discuss what's on my mind until we can all three of us sit down together.'

'Well that'll be a while, if I know my elder two. Thankfully, Sam's a contented little boy, different temperament from his brother. He sleeps pretty well. Usually.'

★　★　★

Gavin moved a splodge of macaroni and cheese from his younger son's cheek to his mouth. 'You've eaten almost all of it, Sam. Good boy.'

'Daddy, can we have a pudding? We ate all our peas and carrots.'

Gavin turned to his daughter. 'Half of them, don't you mean?'

'Please, Daddy! Can we, please? There was too many peas.'

'You can take out a yoghurt each for you and Jack from the fridge. Sam's having banana custard.'

'I'll get it.' Sophie scrambled off her chair. 'I think Mummy's back!'

'We're home,' Tina's voice called from the hall.

Sophie surged across the kitchen, leaving the fridge door open. 'Have you brought Nana?'

'I'm here, Sophie.' Molly closed the front door behind her and bent down to hug her granddaughter. 'Have you all been good since I saw you last?'

Sophie put her head on one side. 'Sometimes a bit bad, I think. Especially Jack.'

'Sophie, have you finished your tea?' asked her mother.

Gavin called from the kitchen, 'Between courses. Hullo Molly. Come in, if you dare!'

Sophie grabbed her nana's hand. 'Come and sit with us.'

Molly, pulled along, entered the kitchen with a feeling of warmth and delight at being there.

Gavin stood up and gave her a hug. 'See who's here, Jack? Sam's mouth is full, or else I'm sure he'd make a welcome speech.'

'Silly Daddy.' Sophie giggled.

'It's all right, Sophie. I've forgiven you for leaving the fridge door open.'

'Maybe the handle needs fixing.' She gave him a winning smile.

Molly hid a grin. 'Don't let me hold up the meal.'

'Not too much left over, I see.' Tina inspected the discarded plates. 'How about something to drink?' She filled the kettle while her mother underwent interrogation by Sophie and Jack.

'Molly's holding up well,' muttered Gavin under his breath as he brought dirty crockery to the draining board.

'Jack's fascinated by planes. He hasn't quite got his head around how all those people fit inside what he thinks looks like a model aircraft in the sky.'

'Your mother looks good, doesn't she?'

Tina hesitated. 'She does, but she had a little episode on holiday.' She glanced across at the table. 'Tell you later. She says she needs to discuss something.'

'So, not in front of the children?'

'Exactly. I have a feeling this has something to do with her evasiveness over our Christmas invitation. Now we have that beautiful house in the Cotswolds booked and Uncle Chris has paid the deposit, if Mum really is plotting something for December, everyone else really needs to know. And fast.'

'Of course.' Gavin wiped his hands. 'Not long to wait.'

'I just hope she hasn't made a commitment she can't break. It's so ironic, given she came back from her hols to discover she no longer has her caring job.'

★ ★ ★

'Shall we sit outside?'

'Just for a while,' said Tina. 'If that's all right with you, Mum?'

'I'll feel as if I'm still on holiday, so let's go for it while we can.'

'An excellent philosophy,' said Gavin, carrying a jug of lemon barley water through to the patio.

Molly looked around her. 'You've done loads since I was last here. It looks lovely. How on earth you find the time, I don't know.'

'Bits here, bits there,' said Tina.

'Gavin sees to the mowing and I try to keep the weeds at bay and find cheap and cheerful bedding plants.'

Molly knew from Tina's speculative look that her daughter expected her to explain what she'd meant earlier in the car. She waited while Gavin filled their glasses.

'The thing is, I'm considering moving house.' She took a swallow of lemon barley water and sat back in her chair but not before noticing Tina's relieved glance at Gavin.

'Well, that's a surprise, Molly. I thought you were a fixture in Black Cove.'

'So did I, Gavin, but a strange thing happened while I was in Madeira.' She looked at Tina. 'Before you ask, this has absolutely nothing to do with my bump on the head.'

'This is what I was going to tell you,' said Tina to Gavin. 'Mum fell back into the swimming pool and almost knocked herself out on the way.'

'I was very quickly rescued and carted off to hospital, but all was well.

Throughout the holiday I was with a pleasant group of people, and I had Kathy's company for meals and outings, but I found myself thinking more and more about my family.'

'In a good way, I hope!' Gavin smiled at his mother-in-law.

'Definitely. And it occurred to me that I'm not much use to any of you while I'm living where I am.'

Tina leaned forward. 'But that's the last home you and Dad made together, Mum. You have all the things around you that you both chose.'

'Worldly goods, yes, but not the most important things. Not my family.' She picked up her glass again. 'Mmm . . . lovely. I'm not daft enough to decide I want to live somewhere halfway between you and Tom. That would be a pointless move. So this is what I've decided — but if you have any objections, speak now or forever hold your peace.' She looked from one to the other. 'I think the time is right to put my cottage on the market and find somewhere smaller — somewhere maybe within a five-mile radius of you two.'

'Wow.' Tina jumped up. 'That's amazing.'

'You're pleased?'

Tina gave Molly a big hug.

'I think you can take that as a yes,' said Gavin. 'It's fantastic news. We'll all of us enjoy having you near.'

'I'll try not to become an interfering mother-in-law!'

'I can't see that happening,' said Gavin. 'Does Tom know?'

'Not yet, darling. I wanted to make sure you both approved of my idea. And don't for one moment think I'd have decided to move to Newcastle if you hadn't given me the thumbs-up. It's a wonderful part of the world, but I like living in the West Country.'

'You'll still be about as far west as you are now, Molly. So no problems there.'

'Have you had the house valued yet?' Tina sat down again.

'I've had two agents come and I've

decided on the one quoting the lowest percentage commission. They both gave me the same figure for the asking price.'

'Are you on the market yet?'

'Gosh, no.' Molly pretended to bite her nails. 'I didn't dare sign anything until I was sure you two approved. I'll be going ahead, as soon as I get back.'

'That'll give us a chance to look around here,' said Tina. 'We can have a look at websites, just as you can do at home, and if you see something you really like we could check it out. Also, I can take you to one or two places you probably haven't visited before.'

'That'd be very helpful.' Molly hesitated. 'All this is why I didn't jump at your kind invitation. The next months are a bit of an unknown quantity, aren't they? If I'm lucky and find a buyer quickly, I could be living in Wales by the time Christmas comes around.'

'You could indeed,' said Gavin.

'On the other hand, if I don't have any luck by autumn, I could still be in Cornwall until the market picks up again next spring.'

'Should that happen,' said Gavin, 'I'm sure you'd find house-hunters have other things on their minds over the Christmas holidays. Even if people don't enjoy or have no cause to celebrate that time of year, they know many others do.'

'I suppose so,' said Molly. 'Anyway, whether I travel from Cornwall or from five miles down the road, I'd love to spend the festive season with you — and thank you both very much for inviting me.'

'Our pleasure,' said Gavin.

Molly noticed the two exchange glances and tried putting two and two together. Tina particularly looked very relieved that her mother would be around in six months' time. Surely there wasn't another happy event in the offing? She decided to say nothing.

*   *   *

With so much else on her mind, Molly hadn't got around to emailing Michael.

It seemed pointless to write to him while he was all those miles away in Canada, moving every one or two nights as his tour group progressed along the eastern seaboard. She'd looked up the itinerary on the holiday company's website and sighed enviously as she read the names . . . Toronto, Niagara Falls, Kingston, Ottawa, Quebec, Montreal. Several of them she'd learned about in her school-days, and Niagara was somewhere she'd visited with her late husband.

She was back home, sale agreement signed and agent's sign planted in her front garden. Friends and neighbours had been ringing or stopping her in the street to ask why she was leaving. It almost reached the point when she wondered that very thing herself.

When they first moved to Cornwall because of John's job, Tom, at eighteen, had been about to begin his gap year. Tina hadn't taken kindly to moving schools but luckily was befriended by someone whose best friend had moved to another area. When Tina followed in her brother's footsteps and went to university, she'd met Gavin. Tom took much longer to settle down but the rambling old cottage had housed lots of visitors, young and old, and contained many happy memories.

Molly remembered how much elbow grease she and her late husband needed to refurbish the tired property they'd bought for a realistic price, reflecting its shabby condition. But it had proved to be a sturdy house and now, looking round at her creams and pale apricot and coffee shades, offset by shiny white gloss paintwork, she felt proud to show off her home to prospective purchasers.

She wandered into the kitchen to make herself a drink. She had an hour to go before the first viewing she'd ever experienced on her own. It seemed the perfect opportunity to compose an email to Michael. It would be embarrassing if he suddenly realised he hadn't heard from her and rang her again. Any excuse she gave for not emailing him as promised would seem lame, and she didn't want that.

Molly hadn't lost her touch-typing skills. Her fingers flew over the keyboard as she described her visit to Wales and confirmed her decision to sell her cottage and move nearer her daughter. She stopped to recall the names of the scattering of small towns and villages Tina had shown her and told him she'd fallen for Haverstone, the nearest town, which, compared with her present location, seemed like a metropolis. No doubt that would amuse someone who lived within striking distance of the lively Welsh capital.

She told Michael she'd prefer to live within walking distance of the town centre, as she had no car nowadays. Tina and Gavin lived four or five miles outside the town that was Gavin's base and, in the rare event of him managing to take a lunch break, he'd be able to pop in for a snack.

She'd just sent the message when the doorbell rang, making her jump, although she had her eye on the time.

In a twinkling, Molly hid her coffee mug inside the fridge, rather than have it sully her spotless sink and draining board. John would have chuckled at that if he'd been there to see it. But he wasn't, and she needed to act like the responsible woman she was and do her best to help achieve a sale.

She welcomed the negotiator and a couple she thought to be in their early forties. They seemed to like the house and thanked her very charmingly, but Molly was left feeling deflated when she closed her front door behind them.

She wandered outside. Her neighbour, collecting her washing, called over the wall. If Molly stood on tiptoe she could just about see Amy.

'How did the viewing go?'

'Hard to tell,' said Molly. 'They seemed impressed. Said all the right things. But that might be the last I see of them.'

'I know how you feel,' said Amy. 'But I do understand your decision to move. That garden's too big for you to look after all on your own.' Hastily she added, 'Although you do an excellent job.'

'Thanks.' Molly grinned. 'But you're right. I can do without a big garden these days.'

The sound of her phone ringing took her attention. 'Sorry, Amy. Speak soon.'

She hurried inside and grabbed the receiver just as her answer phone kicked in. Maybe the estate agent was ringing with news of another viewing. 'Sorry, Molly Reid here,' she said, hoping she hadn't cut short her conversation only to find herself greeting a cold caller.

'Well, that's good.'

She recognised the voice and suddenly felt quite pink and breathless. 'Goodness! I've only just emailed you.'

'And I've only just read your message. Thank you so much for telling me your news.'

'Not at all. It's all a bit scary, but I think I've made the right decision.'

'I hope I'm not interrupting your first viewing.'

'You're not. The people didn't hang

about, though I'm trying not to read anything into that. But, enough of me. How was Canada?'

'A wonderful experience, even better than my previous trip, I think. Good group of folk. Weather excellent in the main. I'm off back to Madeira this weekend.'

'Same hotel as before?'

'Yes.'

'Please give my best regards to that nice young waiter, Lucas. And to Joana, of course.'

'The receptionist? I'll certainly do that, but I'm not sure I approve of acting as a go-between for you and Lucas.' He chuckled.

'The poor young man will probably wonder who on earth you mean if you do send my best wishes.'

'Doubtful. That particular hotel has a first-class team. Anyway, I'll give him your best wishes. But the reason I'm ringing is to say please tell me when you're planning to visit Wales again, and this time I'll do my best to be around.'

He paused. 'If you'd still like to meet up, that is.'

'That would be lovely. It could take a while before I receive an offer on my cottage, but I live in hope.'

'I imagine, having taken this important decision, you wish everything would go through smoothly now.'

'Have you been in this position too?'

'Oh yes. After my wife — well, you know what I'm saying, Molly.'

'How long?'

'Three years. I waited a year before I moved closer to my son. I'm fortunate to be still working, of course.'

'Especially with a job like yours. I'm very jealous.'

'It's not all glamorous, as you know. Before I forget, I'm relieved there were no ill effects after that bump on the head.'

'If it's not things that go bump in the night, it's things that go bump in the pool!'

She heard his laughter. He'd mentioned some amusing and bizarre nocturnal incidents he'd dealt with over the years and she knew he understood her comment. Again she felt that warm bubble of happiness. Michael had been on his own for only a little longer than she had, and now she felt they might be on the brink of a wonderful friendship. More than that, she didn't want to consider.

Strangely, he appeared to pick up this thought. 'Well you've enough on your mind for now, but let's keep in touch and I'll cross my fingers all goes well. At least you have some idea where you'd like to settle.'

'I'm keeping an eye on suitable properties, but the trouble with that is if I set my heart on one and my house isn't sold, I'm inviting disappointment.'

'It's always a stressful time. I'll be thinking of you. Speak soon, Molly.'

Unlike the first time he'd rung, she felt far more certain why he wanted to keep in touch. Though with his hectic schedule and her going to and fro, she was reminded of that lovely, poignant song, 'Bring In The Clowns'.

Tina found a parking space across the road from the house she and her mother were about to view.

'We're a few minutes early. No harm in peeking at it from outside while we wait.'

'I still can't believe things are moving so quickly. The cottage has only been on the market a month, but as Gavin says, I mustn't count my chickens.'

'No, but if your sale does go through smoothly, you mustn't feel pressured to make a hasty decision. We can find room for you for as long as it takes to buy your new home.'

'You and Gavin have been brilliant. I hope it won't come to putting my furniture in storage, but it's comforting to know I can stay with you if necessary.'

'I'm sure you'll be doing the odd thing for us along the way.'

Molly chuckled. 'Maybe.' She reached across and squeezed her daughter's hand.

'That car that's just arrived could be the agent's.'

They watched a man in a dark suit leave the vehicle and head up the drive to Number 42.

'The outside looks just as good as it did in the photographs,' Tina said as she followed her mother up the pathway.

Molly pressed the doorbell. 'Here we go then. Let's see if the inside lives up to expectations.'

A woman opened the dark blue front door to them and Molly stepped inside, responding to the vendor's cheerful greeting. Experiencing a swift feeling that she'd come home gave Molly an unexpected yet very welcome surprise.

9

Reunion of Friends

She explained her feelings to Michael a few weeks later when they met for lunch. They sat in a quiet corner of the oak-beamed restaurant, enjoying glasses of elderflower cordial while waiting for their homemade soup to be served.

'I'm sorry it's taken such a long time to get together,' said Michael. 'I was afraid you wouldn't be able to make it, given you're on a whistle-stop tour.'

'We're both here now, that's the main thing. I really had to come and walk around my new abode to plan where my furniture would best fit and measure for curtains — stuff like that.'

'From what you tell me, things are going well with the sale of your cottage.'

'Contracts are to be exchanged very soon. As for the new house, I'm crossing my fingers the purchase will go through in time so I don't have to put my furniture into storage.'

'A lot has happened since your holiday.' He sat back as bowls of leek and potato soup arrived. The waitress offered a basket of warm rolls and chunks of French stick and hurried off.

Michael leaned across the table. 'I've been wondering whether you'll be totally tied up with your new house and family over the Christmas period.'

Molly buttered a chunk of wholemeal roll. 'Unless I'm temporarily lodging at my daughter's, I don't know how much time I'll be spending with them. All she's said is that I must keep a week free. But that was before I put my cottage on the market. If I'm living in Wales by the time the winter solstice comes around, I expect I'll be staying maybe for the three nights. How about you?'

'I don't want to sound like Johnny No-mates, as they say, but my son and his wife are spending the holiday in

Spain with friends. Good luck to them, I say. They can do with the break.'

'I imagine you won't be looking for winter sunshine. But does that mean you'll be on your own?'

'It does. I'm looking forward to catching up with some boxed sets and DVDs and books that have sat around for months, waiting for me to have time to enjoy them.'

Molly bit her lip. 'I wish I could invite you to join us, but it's Tina who'll be putting the whole thing together.'

'I couldn't possible intrude,' he cut in. 'You're very kind, Molly. I'm not working again until February, so maybe some time in the New Year we could meet? Perhaps spend a day together? I'd love to catch up with a show, so how about a visit to Cardiff?'

'That sounds lovely.' She looked up from her soup and smiled at him.

Michael held her gaze. 'I enjoy having you in my life, Molly.'

She nodded. 'I was looking forward to seeing you today.'

'If only we had longer together.'

She wished she'd grown too old to blush but felt her cheeks heat. 'Maybe next time we will.'

He raised his glass to her. 'I'll drink to that. And if I can help with your move, please don't hesitate to ask. I know you don't drive, so if it proves difficult for your son-in-law to fetch you, I'll happily help.'

She felt a wave of happiness. How lovely was that? Molly sat back in her chair and gazed at him. 'But that would take you ages, Michael. Thank you very much indeed, but I couldn't possibly impose on you.'

'Look at it this way. If you'll allow me to transport you, we'll have hours together. We'll learn more about each other. I don't need to spell it out, Molly, do I?'

★　★　★

Tina drove her mother to the railway station next morning. 'Next time I meet your train, it'll be because you're travelling from Cornwall to your new home.'

Molly cleared her throat. 'I'm not sure I'll be taking the train.'

'Mum . . . ?'

'Nothing's finalised yet, of course, but Michael has offered to collect me and drive me either to yours or to my new house. Hopefully the latter! Isn't that kind?'

'Kind! Mum, are you sure this isn't a marriage proposal?'

'I knew you'd say something like that. But we're friends, that's all. We're each of us single at a significant time of life and we've struck up a very pleasant relationship. Companionship, I'd call it.'

'Hmm.' Tina drummed the fingers of one hand on the steering wheel. 'I've been wondering when to say this to you, but maybe this is the time. It involves our Christmas plans.'

'If you'd rather it was just the five of you celebrating, you don't need to worry about me, love.'

'Sometimes you're too independent for your own good, Mum. No way are you going to be left on your own. The truth is, Gavin and I are taking you and the children away for a week.'

Molly's head swivelled round. She saw Tina's lips twitch but her daughter kept her eyes focussed on the road.

'Taking us away? But why would you do that?'

'You'll find out when the time comes. It was Gav's idea, so you can blame him. At the time he suggested it, you hadn't even put your house on the market; you were still out in Funchal. But we've made the booking now, so don't you dare go and elope or decide you want to be on your own.' She shot her mother a mutinous look.

'Goodness. Well that's told me. But you must let me contribute.'

'You can supervise the catering if you like.'

Molly chuckled. 'We'll see nearer the time. I'll happily do the cooking, but I can't possibly let you pay for me.' She glanced across at Tina. 'We're almost at the station. Am I allowed to know where we'll be going?'

'Definitely not. Gavin would never forgive me. We haven't told the children yet, but it'll make a difference to Sophie and Jack knowing you'll be with us.'

'But if you've booked us into a hotel, it'll make a difference to what I pack.'

Tina indicated left and drove through the station entrance. 'Um, let me have a think and I'll email you. Right now I need to find a parking space.'

'Just drop me off, love. Don't worry about parking.'

'You're my mum, not a package! I can see a place over there, so no more arguments.'

She didn't argue, and gave Tina an extra-big hug as they parted company on the platform when the train pulled in.

Molly settled into her seat and thought about all that had happened in the three days she'd been staying in Wales. She'd finalised her thoughts about her prospective new home. She'd met up with Michael and discovered, to her astonishment, that he was feeling the same about her as she was about him, though she hadn't dared confess as much to Tina. His offer to drive her all the way from her cottage to her new home was a very significant one. Also, she'd a sneaky feeling that when it came to closing the front door on her old life, there might be a few tears. Having Michael there would be a tangible reminder of her new life and held the possibility of her future including him.

As for Tina's unexpected invitation to join them on some kind of mystery trip, she wasn't too sure how she felt about that. Wouldn't it be better for the children to be at home, with all their familiar toys plus the new gifts Santa Claus would bring?

When she heard her mobile phone bleep and she retrieved it from her pocket, she was touched to find a text from Michael.

10

New Beginning

Molly looked at the clock on Michael's dashboard as soon as she recognised the road sign. 'We've taken about four hours, not counting our lunch stop.'

'On a scale of ten, how excited are you?'

She thought for a few moments. 'Eleven.' She glanced across and saw his lips twitch. 'Okay, I do still feel a wee bit sad.'

'You coped very well, leaving the cottage. I thought it best to keep nattering away about this and that.' He broke off as the voice of his navigational system announced they'd reached their destination.

'I knew what you were up to, and you were so right. It gave me a chance to gather myself together,' said Molly.

'And there's Tina, hopefully with my house keys. I texted her as instructed.'

Tina beckoned to Michael to drive straight onto the hard standing Molly knew would be useful when she had visitors. As soon as Michael switched off his engine, Molly squeezed his hand. 'Thank you so much,' she said.

'My pleasure.'

Tina opened the passenger door and held out a small bunch of keys. 'All in order. Did you have a good journey?'

'Brilliant!' Molly turned to Michael. 'This is my daughter, Tina.'

'Michael, I can't thank you enough for bringing my mother here safe and sound. It can't have been easy for her, leaving Cornwall.'

'Don't set me off again.' But Molly was smiling.

'I'm very pleased to meet you, Tina,' said Michael. 'It's very kind of you to offer me a bed for the night.'

'No problem. I'm afraid the room's not very spacious. We stole part of the biggest bedroom for our baby son, but at least we have somewhere for guests to stay.'

'I've developed the knack of sleeping wherever I lay my head.' Michael's eyes twinkled.

'That must be an asset in the kind of work you do.' Tina turned to Molly. 'You'll be in Sophie's room, Mum. She's sleeping in Jack's bottom bunk. I thought I'd deny you that privilege.'

Molly laughed. 'Whatever you say. It's a good job I like pink!'

'Come on then,' said Tina. 'Your big moment has arrived.'

Molly took the keys from Tina and looked at her new front door. 'I must make a wish.' She unlocked and pushed the door open. 'Goodness, two cards have arrived!' She picked up the envelopes. 'One's from Tom and Lucy. I think the other is from Kathy. How kind!'

'Sophie and Jack are still working on ours,' said Tina. 'Now, how about you give the tour guide a tour of your new home?'

'I seem to have done nothing but pack and unpack over the last months,' Molly spoke out loud as she pulled her suitcase out of the wardrobe.

She found it hard to believe it was the 22nd of December, the day before she was due to travel with Tina and family to an unknown destination. She'd made a list of things to pack because she daren't risk forgetting anything and, apart from everything necessary for a week away in the UK in December, she had certain high-priority items:

Gifts for family — nothing bulky (as advised by Tina)

A stunning dress for Christmas Day — something sparkly if possible (also advised by Tina)

Two aprons (if Molly insisted on helping in the kitchen)

Favourite DVDs for holiday watching

Books (ditto)

Sensible walking shoes plus wellies to

throw in the boot (no pun intended, added by Tina)

Specs and mobile phone

Laptop?

Molly decided not to bother with the latter. If they spoke to Tom and Lucy on Christmas Day they would use Gavin's. Anyway, Tina had one of those phones that did everything bar make you a cup of tea. Molly had posted her gifts to Newcastle well in advance, and the presents had also been delivered to Helen and Chris. Goodness knew when her nephew Dave would turn up. His job involved a lot of travelling, but her sister thought her son might be around for Christmas, though Dave was quite likely to change his plans at the last minute.

Molly had everything piled on the bed ready to pack. Her old but oh-so-comfortable hiking boots plus posh floral wellies, which Sophie would no doubt try on, stood beside the front door. But now as she looked at the dress she'd selected, she wasn't sure. Its material was a clingy jersey fabric and she thought the red suited her colouring. Tiny seed pearls enhanced the neckline, and she'd chosen pearl stud earrings when she wore the dress on holiday for the group dinner. On that occasion Michael had commented on her appearance, and that was the first time she'd looked at him as someone other than the pleasant person wearing a name badge and carrying a small attaché case.

The decision was made. In went the red dress. Maybe she'd wear it again if they took that trip to Cardiff he'd suggested.

*   *   *

'Are we nearly there yet?'

'I don't know, sweetheart. You'll have to ask your daddy.'

'Not much longer, everyone,' said Gavin. 'We'll stop at the next services, then leave the motorway and be there well before it's dark.'

Molly thought she'd guessed their destination. She hadn't been to the Cotswolds in years but suspected that was where they were heading.

'Do you know where we're staying, Nana?'

'No, Sophie. Your mummy and daddy are making me wait and see. It's fun, isn't it?'

'Not if Father Christmas can't find us.'

'Oh, I'm sure the elves will sort it all out. It's a very magical time of year. Lots of surprises and lovely things happening.'

'Father Christmas must have sat nav for his sleigh, surely?'

Molly watched Gavin and Tina exchange smiles. Children these days took so much for granted. Sometimes she wondered if her two elder grandchildren thought of their nana as someone to be pitied, given her lack of interest in computer games and the various gizmos they had in their lives.

'I'm hungry,' said Jack. 'Shall I wake

up Sam and ask him if he's hungry too?'

'Best not, Jack,' said his mother, turning round. 'If you ask Nana nicely, she might find you a banana in our emergency rations.'

Molly never failed to be impressed by the way Tina prepared for a car journey. But she had a sneaking suspicion both Tina and Gavin were a tiny bit on edge. Maybe, as they still hadn't told her whether they were heading for a hotel or self-catering accommodation, they wondered if Molly might have preferred to know her destination. She didn't mind being surprised, but she still wondered what the two elder children would make of their temporary new home.

'There's the sign for the services,' said Gavin. 'We'll soon be able to stretch our legs. I'll carry Sam if he's still asleep.'

When they all piled out of the car, pulling on their jackets, Tina took Sophie and Jack each by the hand and headed for the play area. Molly and Gavin were about to go into the services when Molly noticed Sam waking up. At the same time, Gavin's mobile phone rang.

'Let me take him for you.' She held out her arms.

'Thanks, Molly.' He checked who was calling and moved slightly away from her.

Gavin held the phone to his ear, a big grin spreading across his face. Molly was talking to Sam and pointing to where his brother and sister were playing on the swings. She could hear her son-in-law's voice but, engrossed with the baby, had no idea who was keeping him chatting.

When he closed the call and walked back to Molly, Tina was bringing the children to join them.

'Sorry about that,' said Gavin. 'Let's go inside and get ourselves a hot drink and something to keep the munchies at bay.'

He took little Sam from Molly and the elder two immediately each grabbed one of their grandmother's hands. Their parents walked behind.

'Tom rang,' Gavin spoke quietly. 'Lucy's driving and they were heading for these services to take a break, would you believe.'

'Oh no! How far away are they?'

'Don't worry. He knows somewhere else they can stop. He did his research well, because they're heading for the place before this one if you're southbound.'

'Phew,' said Tina, 'that's a relief.'

'I told him we were actually here and we daren't risk bumping into them — not when we've kept this secret from Molly all this time.'

'That would've been an anticlimax,' said Tina. 'So, as we've already agreed, whoever arrives at Halliday House first can ring the owners and one of them will be there within five minutes. Okay?'

Before Gavin could respond, her phone rang. 'What now, I wonder,' said Gavin.

'Hang on.' Tina pulled out her mobile. She mouthed *Aunty Helen* and accepted the call.

Gavin caught up with Molly as they approached the entrance. 'Loos first, or café?'

'I'll take Sophie to the ladies' room while you wait for Tina, shall I? She seems to be taking a while on the phone.'

'Thanks. I'll just hang on here with the boys until Tina's finished. It might be something to do with accessing our accommodation.'

Molly decided to say nothing and left Gavin to wait for his wife. Tina still stood outside, her face serious as she listened. But he didn't have long to wait before she was back at his side.

'I'm afraid we're going to be minus one person over Christmas.'

'I hope no one's ill. But I need to take Jack to the toilet. You can tell me what's happened in a bit.'

She took Sam from his father's arms. 'Helen says Dave's pulled out. Something about a whirlwind trip to Madrid.'

Gavin grabbed Jack's hand. 'That means we have one spare room, doesn't it?'

'We can always split Sophie and Jack up.'

But Gavin's thoughts were whizzing. Revolving around Molly. He'd taken a liking to her friend Michael when the tour guide stayed with them and saw no reason why Tom and Lucy and the others shouldn't approve. Molly had mentioned Michael would be spending the whole of the holiday alone. Perhaps he'd like to take over Dave's place. Presumably Molly had Michael's number saved on her phone, and she of course must be the one to agree the idea. He decided to run the suggestion past Tina first.

'How about this for an plan? But it's entirely up to your mother, of course.'

11

Here Comes Christmas

'How strange.' Molly peered at the dark blue saloon parked on the gravel as Gavin steered his estate car up the drive of Halliday House. 'Isn't that car the same make and colour as Tom's?'

'Is it?' Tina shook her head. 'They had a red one last time we saw them.'

'That was ages ago, but of course this one can't possibly be his.' Molly leaned forward. 'Gavin, are you quite certain your navigation system hasn't got its wires crossed? This place has no hotel sign and it looks more like a manor house to me.'

Tina turned around. 'We're in the right place, Mum,' she said gently. 'Halliday House is our home for the next week. It's part of the Christmas surprise we've prepared.'

'Goodness. I really don't know what

to say. Isn't it rather large for us?'

'Let's get everyone out and inside the house before we worry about unloading our stuff.' Both Tina and Gavin opened their doors and got out.

'We'll go up to the front door together,' said Tina.

'Oh, it's all right, Sam. No one's going to leave you behind.' Gavin detached the car seat and lifted the protesting youngest member of the party out.

Jack was scrunching his feet into the gravel. Molly stood on the driveway, hand in hand with her granddaughter. 'You'll be able to pretend you're a princess in these lovely surroundings, Sophie. I should have packed my diamond tiara.'

'You are funny, Nana.' Sophie giggled.

Before Molly could raise the brass knocker or tug the bell pull, the imposing crimson-painted front door began to open slowly.

'Not today, thank you,' said a male voice.

'Uncle Tom!' Sophie ran forward and her uncle scooped her up and swung her round in the doorway.

'My word, Sophie, you're much heavier than you look when we meet on Skype.' He put her down. 'Well, come on in, everybody. We've only been here twenty minutes ourselves.'

Molly stepped forward and Tom gave her a big hug. 'I hope those are tears of joy at seeing me,' he teased her.

'I thought that looked like your car,' she said triumphantly. 'You've all been plotting and I couldn't be more delighted.' Suddenly she caught sight of the tall fir tree standing in an alcove. The only decorations upon its dark green branches were strands of gleaming tinsel and tiny fairy lights twinkling in a festive starburst.

A smiling Lucy appeared from a doorway, hand in hand with Melissa who had her thumb in her mouth. The little girl gave everyone a suspicious look and turned her face against her mother's legs until Sophie knelt down beside her and gave her a kiss.

Gavin watched children and adults

hugging and kissing and greeting each other. He and Tom exchanged big grins.

'It's going to be chaos, mate,' Gavin said cheerfully. 'But this is what Christmas is all about.'

Tom gave his brother-in-law a pretend punch. 'You bet! Now Mrs Halliday, who brought the keys over, is really pleasant. She told us she'd put basics in the fridge and two bottles of wine in the rack, to wish us a happy time. She and her husband live very close, so any problems, we're to contact them immediately.'

'Great stuff. Look at your mum's face.'

Molly was cuddling Melissa in her arms, her expression one of pure delight. She glanced at her son and son-in-law and laughed out loud. 'You're both very naughty, but I'm thrilled to bits.'

'Well, I'm dying for a cuppa,' said Tom. 'We were so close, we decided not to stop at that other services in the end. Did you realise I'd rung Gavin to say we were planning to call at the services where you'd just arrived?'

Molly looked blank.

'She didn't have the foggiest,' said Gavin. He turned to Molly. 'That was why I waited for Tina to get off the phone while you took Sophie to the ladies' room.'

'You young folk are on your phones so much, I don't take much notice, to be honest.'

'Mum, if you think we're attached to our mobiles, just you wait until your grandchildren get older,' said Tom, giving his mother a quick hug round the shoulders. 'Now I'll go and make a big pot of tea, then I'll help you unload, Gavin. The girls can sort out who's in which bedroom.'

'I've brought an enormous fish pie for supper,' said Lucy. 'It's travelled fine in the car boot. And I've got all the items on my list, Tina.'

'Brilliant,' said Tina. 'You and I can pop out tomorrow and buy the other stuff we'll need.'

'The turkey will be delivered in the morning, as arranged by Mrs Halliday,' said Lucy.

'That checklist she emailed was a

brilliant idea.' Gavin smiled at Molly. 'We daren't bring too much stuff in case you became suspicious.'

'But we've each brought boxes of crackers and party poppers.' Lucy grinned. 'Sorry about the latter, folks. You know what Tom's like.'

'We can't do without party poppers!' Tom grinned. 'More importantly, Lucy and Tina have each made a Christmas cake and of course, we've brought the gifts you posted to us, Ma.'

'For once, I'm speechless,' said Molly. 'It's as if my children have turned into secret agents.'

When the doorbell rang half an hour later, Gavin and Tina exchanged glances.

'Mum? Would you go and see who that is, please?'

Molly looked at her daughter. 'What else have you been up to, young lady? I hope you haven't spent money on flowers?'

'I've no idea what you mean,' said Tina.

Molly hurried into the hallway and opened up the door. As they were in a village she wondered about carol singers, although she couldn't hear any sounds.

'Room for two little ones?' Helen asked.

Molly took one look at her sister and burst into tears.

'That'll get Helen going,' said Uncle Chris as both women fell into each other's arms.

'Well, what else would you expect, Chris? Now, come in out of the cold,' said Molly, brushing away tears trickling down her cheeks. 'I'm still in a state of shock from finding Tom and the others here. This is so amazing. What a wonderful Christmas it's going to be.'

'We're thrilled to be here,' said Helen. 'With our offspring otherwise occupied, we probably would have made do with a roast chicken and a couple of days watching black and white films.'

'But where's your dog?' Tina came to hug the new arrivals. 'Do you want to get her out of the car, Uncle Chris?'

He shook his head. 'Rosie's with our next-door neighbours. They enjoy having her and once they knew we were going away, they offered to look after her.'

'It would've been great to bring her,' said Helen. 'But we thought it might be too much. She's not used to being around little people and she can get a bit crotchety these days.'

'Like you and me, dear!' Chris grinned at his wife.

Tom, ignoring taunts about bossy teachers, called to everyone to claim their rooms. Tina and Lucy had stuck Post-it notes on the doors so everyone knew where they were.

Gavin caught Molly before she could ask about luggage. 'I'll carry your case upstairs in a minute, but first I need to ask you something.'

'What's that?'

'It's a great pity Dave can't be with us, don't you think?'

'Of course. But I'm sure he'll have a fabulous time with his girlfriend and her parents. Helen thinks he'll probably propose to his young lady on Christmas Day. She says she had one of her premonitions.'

'I never knew he was such a

romantic. Premonition or not, that's brilliant news but, as he's not joining us, that leaves one room vacant.'

'I suppose so.'

'That seems a little wasteful, especially when you think of Michael, spending the holiday all on his own. Didn't you tell us his son wouldn't be around, or have I got my wires crossed?'

Molly swallowed hard. 'No, you're quite right. Michael is spending the holiday on his own.' She'd been thinking of him. Wondering whether to ring and tell him she was in the Cotswolds. Finally deciding it might be a little tactless to rave about the wonderful surprise her family had arranged for her.

'Oh goodness,' she said. 'Are you suggesting we should invite him? Isn't it rather short notice?'

'That's up to him to decide, don't you think? Be honest, now, Molly. Would you like him to be here?'

Molly didn't need to think too hard to answer that particular question, but she bit her lip.

'There are the others to consider. Tom and Lucy and Helen and Chris mightn't like the idea of a stranger joining us.'

'Well, he's met all our lot and he seemed to get on fine with the kids. I've already consulted Tom and he said he'd run it by Lucy and the others. If everyone's happy, you can go ahead and invite him.'

'I keep welling up. You'll have to give me a minute.'

'Women,' said Gavin, hugging his mother-in-law. 'Off you go and talk to Tom while I bring our luggage indoors. Then we can settle down by the fire, if that's not being too optimistic?'

Left alone, Molly dabbed her eyes again and told herself not to be such a wimp. She hoped Michael wouldn't think she was being too forward, ringing him with an invitation to join a family Christmas. But he could always say no. If he did, she'd understand. But now, with everyone knowing she was going to ask him, she suddenly felt shy.

'You two missed the first tea round,

Helen,' she called. 'I'll go and make some more.'

In the kitchen with her son, she busied herself taking cups and saucers from a cupboard. Tom pointed out a tin of assorted biscuits.

'How do you like your surprise, Ma?'

'It's fantastic. I couldn't be more thrilled. The very fact that we're all together for Christmas is a gift in itself.'

'I hadn't realised your tour guide friend is actually a little more than a friend, isn't he?'

Whoops. Molly kept her tone light. 'Michael's become a good friend, Tom. He's an extremely kind man and I know you'd get on well with him.'

'Maybe. It's your life, Ma. If you want him here with us, I'm not going to stand in your way.'

'It's not my party,' said Molly. 'I wouldn't have brought the matter up, but Gavin's made this suggestion and I rather like the idea. Michael and I aren't starry-eyed teenagers. We're both on our own and we very much enjoy one another's company.'

She shrieked as Tom suddenly lifted her off her feet and whirled her round. 'Put me down, Tom! You haven't done that since you were nineteen.'

He returned her to floor level. 'I didn't want you thinking I was an old misery, begrudging you some fun.'

'I shall have plenty of fun with all you lot around. Michael isn't as blessed as I am. The question is, are you sure you're happy with a stranger joining us?'

'But he's not a stranger, is he? He's met half the gang already.'

Tina appeared in the doorway. 'Thumbs up! Everyone thinks it's a great idea.' She hesitated. 'Tom? Everything all right?'

'Absolutely, sis. It'll be great to have another bloke around, especially if he plays golf.'

Molly pulled her handbag towards her and took out her phone. 'Well, there's no time like the present. I'll see if I can contact him.'

Helen came in. 'Oh, what a gorgeous kitchen.'

Sophie followed her. 'I can see a cream pony in a field, through my window! Can I go and say hello?'

Molly thought how lovely it was, seeing everyone catching up with each other's news, hearing sounds of laughter and teasing drift down the staircase. She gave a wry smile as, clutching her phone, she headed for the sitting room to ring Michael from the window seat she'd always fantasised about having in her own home one day. It didn't matter if anyone came in, now all the adults knew about her developing friendship. She called up his number and waited, gazing into the brightness of the log fire that Tom said he'd found set ready for someone to apply a match.

Michael answered just as Molly came close to giving up.

* * *

Molly astonished herself by sleeping in longer than usual. By the time she went downstairs to the kitchen, the darkness of Christmas Eve morning was slowly dissolving. She found her grandchildren and their parents breakfasting at the enormous refectory table. Gavin had got to grips with the catering-sized electric toaster, which gave a satisfying ping, greeting Molly with the comforting aroma of warm toast.

'Here she comes! At least you've beaten Helen and Chris,' said Tom, pulling out a chair.

'Tea or coffee, Molly?' Lucy asked.

'Tea please. I must say you all look very rested.'

'Amazingly. Every child slept through once we got to the witching hour,' said Tina.

'I doubt that's going to happen tonight,' said Gavin. 'Sophie tells me she's going to stay awake so she's ready to greet Santa when he gets to us.'

'Aren't you going to leave your stockings beside the fireplace?'

'I don't know,' Sophie wailed. 'Will that be easier for Father Christmas?'

'I'd say so,' said her father. 'Easier on his poor old legs if he doesn't have to climb the stairs.'

'That's what we'll do then.' Sophie dug her spoon into her porridge.

'What time do you think Michael will arrive?' Tina asked her mother.

Molly took a swallow of tea before answering. She'd been able to pass the good news to the others after a short but satisfactory conversation with Michael the evening before. He'd sounded completely stunned that they should think of inviting him to join the party, but Molly assured him everyone considered it a brilliant idea.

'They're not at all bothered about me being the only one without a partner,' she'd told him candidly. 'It's that they know we've become friendly and they also realise you were quite content to be on your own. So, it's not about feeling sorry for either of us. It's not even a case of an extra pair of hands for the clearing up. There's an all-singing all-dancing dishwasher in the kitchen.'

He'd chuckled at that and assured her he was thrilled to be invited and it wasn't at all short notice for someone who held pride of place in the *Guinness Book of Records* for the speediest ever packing of a suitcase.

'He said he thought the journey would take him about an hour and three quarters,' she said. 'But he wants to stop off in Fylechester on the way.'

'I hope you told him no one expects gifts,' said Tom. 'Having to sort that would reduce the poor man to a gibbering wreck!'

'Oh, I told him gifts weren't necessary. Knowing him, he probably wants to pick up something edible or maybe a bottle or two. Heaven help our waistlines after all the goodies we'll be putting away.'

'Which reminds me,' said Tina. 'You and I need to go shopping soon, Lucy. We still have last-minute things to buy. But someone needs to be here for the man bringing the turkey. And it goes without saying you need to be here to let Michael in, Mum.'

'He didn't anticipate arriving until

early afternoon,' said Molly. 'We're not to wait for lunch, in case he's held up.'

'Lunch?' said Gavin. 'How about leaving that to the men today?'

Molly didn't miss the happy look passing between Lucy and Tina. 'It sounds like a good offer. You two have your eye on that portable barbeque, don't you?'

'You bet,' said Tom. 'Mrs Halliday showed it to us yesterday. It's under cover with all the bits we need nearby, so if we can get sausages and maybe a few burgers and bake some potatoes in the range, we'll be well away.'

'A barbeque in December will certainly be a first for me.' Molly held up her plate so Gavin could place two perfect slices of grilled bread on it.

'We can all wrap up warm, and there's a table beneath the covered part of the patio. Or, people can bring their food into the kitchen.'

'Would you like that, children?' Lucy gently steered the spoon in her daughter's hand towards her mouth rather than her button nose.

'Yes, please,' said Sophie.

'Sausages — yay!' Jack nodded his head.

'Would you like me to make soup for this evening? Something easy, like vegetable, maybe?'

'Fantastic, Mum. If you check out what's already here before we go shopping, we can get whatever it is you need,' said Tina.

'Your soups are always wonderful,' said Lucy.

'Thanks, Lucy. Let's hope the little ones agree.'

'Have we missed breakfast?' Helen and Chris appeared in the doorway.

'I'll say,' said Tom. 'Unless Melissa's left you some cold porridge.'

'Ignore him, Helen,' said his wife. 'There's freshly made coffee and tea. Gavin's on toast duty and the cereals are on the worktop.'

'Any leftover porridge, Chris will demolish,' said Helen. 'We'll look after ourselves then you can give us jobs. I

196

imagine there's plenty to do.'

'We haven't got a roster, Auntie,' said Tina. 'But do you think you could help keep an eye on the children while Lucy and I go shopping?'

Chris turned around from the microwave, where he was warming a bowl of porridge. 'We could make a den in the games room. Maybe use it as our spaceship. What do you think, Jack and Sophie?'

'Can I be a space princess, Uncle Chris?' Sophie's face lit up.

'Definitely.'

'That's a lovely idea,' said Molly. 'But before you take off, it would be good if you could help me decorate the little tree I brought with me.'

'That's done good service, Ma,' said Tom. 'Some of those miniature ornaments must be thirty or more years old.'

'Much more than that in some cases,' said Molly. 'I used to buy one or two new ones every year.'

'Nana's special baby tree used to sit

in a pot on the table every Christmas when Uncle Tom and I were little,' Tina explained to Sophie and Jack.

'It's a memory tree as well as a decoration,' said Helen, reaching for the jar of honey.

'Well, yes,' said Molly. 'And this year, it's also a happy tree because all of us are spending Christmas together for the first time in ages.'

12

Last-minute Preparations

Michael arrived in Fylechester around ten o'clock and, avoiding the car park, found a space to leave his car down a side street. He had a roomy canvas satchel in which to put his purchases. His breath made puffs of smoke in the cold, crisp air and he was glad of the long woollen scarf wound around his neck which, according to his son, turned him into Doctor Who, though Michael couldn't recall which one.

Molly had told him not even to think about buying gifts for everyone, but he wanted to find small items for the children's stockings and token presents for the adults. Except for Molly. He already had something for Molly — something he'd spotted in a quaint little shop in Quebec's French Quarter on his first trip to Canada after they'd met in Madeira. He'd allocated his tour group two and a half hours and some had gone off to explore the cathedral's rich colours, curves and carvings, while others opted for a leisurely cruise along the St Lawrence River.

He'd known the most likely place to find what he wanted, although at that point he couldn't have explained exactly what it was. One particular shop had attracted him, but he stood gazing into the window until one piece of jewellery seemed to speak to him. Inside, cupping the item in the palm of his hand, he knew his instinct was right and that the jewellery was perfect for Molly. He'd hung on to it, telling himself he was probably out of line even to imagine she might share the kind of feelings he had about her.

Now he couldn't believe how much fun he was having, and he hadn't even arrived at Halliday House yet. He'd bought little tubs of bubble stuff, a yellow car with a satisfying flashing light for Jack, a sparkling bracelet and tiara set fit for a princess called Sophie, a soft and squishy white monkey and a stripy tiger for the younger children, plus foil-wrapped milk chocolate fish and cars. He knew little people shouldn't be given too much sugar, so he'd make sure their parents had the last word on that one.

He bought a double pack of playing cards and old-style metal puzzles for the men. They could always swap with each other if necessary. As for Molly's daughter and daughter-in-law, well, he didn't have a clue what their tastes were but took a chance and purchased two glorious soft woollen scarves, one in palest powder blue and one in a shade of pink that he thought might be raspberry. Again, they could swap them round if they wished. Two bottles of bubbly and a pack of animal-shaped biscuits for the children completed his purchases, except that he stopped off for coffee in a wonderful shop that sold handmade chocolate and bought a box of exquisite truffles. He knew Molly had a sweet tooth and no doubt she'd prefer to take them home rather than share them around, even if Christmas was the season of goodwill.

But he'd forgotten Molly's sister and brother-in-law, so he hurried back to the coffee shop where he bought a tin of French biscuits. A safe option maybe, but even if the couple didn't eat the buttery cookies and crisp hazelnut wafers, they'd have something a little different in the cupboard to offer visitors.

He'd also forgotten about wrapping paper, so he dived into a shop and bought sheets printed with ice-skating teddy bears plus ones bearing scenes of Dickensian carollers and laughing children whizzing about on toboggans. He even remembered to purchase holly-printed sticky tape and a pack of gift tags plus one sheet of silver paper to wrap Molly's special gift. This retail splurge gave him a lot of enjoyment and was much more fun than making the traditional payment from his current account to those of his son and daughter.

As an afterthought and not without hesitation, Michael bought a pack containing two gold and two silver hearts joined to fine chains. They weren't expensive but they looked classy, and he thought Molly might like them for future years as they weren't as big as the normal bauble size and, living on her own, she probably didn't go in for a big fir tree.

At that point, the phrase *living on her own* echoed in his head and he knew exactly what he wanted the New Year to bring. The question was — did she, would she, feel the same?

Michael stowed his shopping in his car and got behind the wheel with a sense of satisfaction. He smiled to himself as his dangling scarf entangled itself around the gear stick, something that probably wouldn't have happened to Doctor Who. But, as if he'd been whisked via the TARDIS, here he was, only twelve miles from his destination, when this time yesterday he was contemplating buying a small chicken to roast for his solitary Christmas dinner. Life was funny like that. Sometimes you jogged along in the same routine. Sometimes you felt as though you were a giant counter in the game he'd often played with his children way back, whooshing down a snake or climbing up a ladder. What would they think if he rang them and said he was celebrating Christmas in the Cotswolds with people he hardly knew? Except for one special lady, of course.

He drove off with a smile on his face, listening to a Radio 2 presenter talking about top festive tunes and carols through the decades. When the first notes of 'Driving Home for Christmas' floated from the speakers, he had to cope with a sudden surge of nostalgia. Of course he wasn't driving home, far from it, but he was driving to be with someone who had become very important to him.

But he also knew he must keep a

sense of perspective. This lovely lady had entered his life but she'd had a lot to contend with since she'd bumped her head on the side of the swimming pool and regained full consciousness to find her tour guide dripping wet and staring down at her. His natural reaction had been to jump in and help whoever was in difficulty; but when he realised he held Molly in his arms, he'd thanked his lucky stars he was close by. That confirmed an inkling of something he'd previously tried to ignore.

Molly's return to Cornwall, only to find she no longer had a job, appeared to have set off a domino fall of events, leading her to sell her home of twenty years and begin a new life in Wales, near her daughter and family. How pleased he'd felt when she agreed to his suggestion that he should drive her to the new abode on the day she said goodbye to her cottage.

Not long after, she'd been whisked away to spend Christmas in the Cotswolds, surrounded by all her close family. In her phone call yesterday, she explained how much of a surprise the Cotswolds trip had been. He'd noted the pleasure and happiness in her voice as she chatted. She'd raised the matter of him joining the party in rather a shy manner. This he liked. He too felt a little shy. He admired Molly's independent nature and the quiet, practical way she dealt with things, but there was also a vulnerability about her that appealed to the protective side of his nature.

Extrovert people were fine and many would say tour guides needed outgoing qualities. But he felt he and Molly were two of a kind. They'd spent very little time together, but something had clicked and these next five or so days would give them an opportunity to learn more about each other. If they parted after the holiday and they both felt a twinge of sadness, wouldn't that indicate the reaching of an important landmark? But as he peered at the next signpost coming up, just as he didn't need a navigation system to guide him to Coln St Peter, he felt convinced his feelings for Molly weren't about to change.

Michael took the left turn at the next road junction and soon he was driving through the pretty little town that was barely more than an overgrown village. He drove past an inn that made him think of old coaching days and roaring log fires. He spotted an antiques shop with a holly wreath on its door, a tearoom that also sold crafts, and one of those stores that, even though it didn't stand on a corner, probably lived up to that title. He didn't need to stop but he noticed a farm shop on the opposite side of the road that appeared to be doing a roaring trade. He couldn't help smiling at the sight of an attractive young woman emerging, carrying a splendid example of Brussels sprouts on the branch.

Michael changed gear ready to turn right immediately after passing St Peter's Church on his left. He needed to follow a winding road for half a mile and then he'd find the gates of Halliday House, also on his left. Thank goodness he was accustomed to meeting strangers and striking up immediate conversations. He had at least already met Molly's daughter and her husband and children.

When he drove through a pair of imposing wrought-iron gates, he noticed Gavin and Tina's sturdy, mud-splattered estate car parked to one side of the drive. One other vehicle was parked at the other side. He pulled in behind Gavin's car, switched off his engine, and allowed peace and quiet to wash over him. His Christmas began here.

13

A Warm Welcome

Molly thought she heard the crackle of gravel beneath tyres while crossing the hallway to check the fire Gavin lit earlier. She preferred a cold, crisp Christmas rather than those murky, muggy ones that sometimes came along. The outside temperature had plummeted to near freezing, although the house remained cosy.

She peered through the window to one side of the front door and her heart gave a little skip, or so it seemed. Michael, looking taller than ever in a long overcoat and a wonderful scarf straight out of *A Christmas Carol*, was walking towards the house. To her amazement, she felt an emotional sugar rush identical to the one she'd experienced upon seeing Tom, Lucy and her little granddaughter the day before.

Molly, head held high, opened the door and remembered to click the latch so she didn't shut herself out. Tom was outside in the play area with all the children except Sam, each one bundled up like a cheerful Christmas parcel. Some sort of ball game was causing loads of shouts and merriment. Gavin was in the kitchen, supervising Sam and making sure the huge pan of soup Molly had prepared for later simmered gently. Tina and Lucy weren't back yet. Helen and Chris, keen walkers, having spent some time with the children, were out exploring.

At once Michael noticed Molly. She saw his face light up. Watched his pace increase. 'Hello! Don't get cold now,' he called.

'I'm so pleased to see you!' Before she'd even thought about it, she ran onto the driveway and into his arms. He hugged her to him. His long woolly scarf tickled her face. He smelt of cedarwood soap.

He kissed her on the cheek. 'I didn't

think we'd be meeting again until well into the New Year. Thank you so much for inviting me here, Molly.' He released his hold and stepped back.

She felt a sense of loss. How silly was that. And how could she have forgotten how blue his eyes were? No time like the present! Molly stood on tiptoe and kissed his lips. 'There. One of us had to make the first move!'

He burst out laughing. 'You're full of surprises, you know that?'

'Are you complaining, Mr Todd?'

'I should say not. Do you think anyone's watching?'

'Whyever would they want to do that?'

He grinned and suddenly she could see the man as he must have looked as a coltish schoolboy, wondering how the heck he could figure out whether the girl he liked would slap his face if he stole a kiss. She closed her eyes as he took her in his arms and their lips met.

He whispered in her ear while he still held on to her as if he'd never let her go. 'I didn't want you to feel as though I was rushing you.'

'I sensed that,' she said, drawing back and raising one hand to smooth his cheek. 'But as soon as I heard my nephew couldn't join us, all I could think of was you and whether you'd think I was a scheming hussy if I invited you here. I didn't want to seem pushy, but fortunately Gavin thought of you and suggested asking if you'd like to join us.'

He took her hands in his. 'Pushy? I like any scheme involving you, Molly.' He held her hands to his face. 'But you're getting cold. Let's go inside before you turn into an ice maiden.'

'Come on then. Gavin's running the kitchen like a drop-in coffee shop and I think he's enjoying himself more than he'd admit.'

'Let's hope the novelty doesn't wear off.'

Molly pushed open the front door.

'What a fantastic house.' Michael gazed around the spacious hallway, his eyes taking in the superb pine tree and lingering on the elegant, sweeping staircase. 'My flip remark about your needing a six-bedroom manor house for a get-together seems to have been prescient.'

'It certainly does. Would you believe there's even a small indoor pool? Gavin and Tom had a quick dip this morning, though we've kept that a secret from the children for now. The door's kept locked of course.'

'I imagine their mums and dads plan on tiring them out later so they get off to sleep quickly. I well remember those days.'

'Me too. But we never stayed anywhere as upmarket as this place. My family are very naughty, spoiling me like this. I still have to pinch myself to make sure I'm really here. Now I shall have to pinch myself twice as hard to make sure you're really here too!'

'Molly, you make me feel young again, you really do! Even if I know my son and daughter would fall about laughing if they heard me say it.'

'I've never thought to enquire your age. Somehow I assumed you were a bit younger than me.'

'So that would make me about 45? Flatterer!'

She laughed. 'We'll talk later. But before you meet all the gang, you have to look at Sophie's decoration. The owners installed the tree and put the lights up but Sophie brought something she made in school. See if you can spot it. She's sure to ask when she comes inside.'

Michael peered at the twinkling lights and the carefully draped strands of tinsel. 'Aha . . . it's the red felt Santa? The homely touch amongst the elegance.'

'That's it. If Sophie asks whether you noticed it, you'll be able to say yes without fibbing.'

He hugged her again.

She turned around and noticed the kitchen door was ajar though there were no sounds from within.

'Let's see how my son-in-law's getting

on.' Molly pushed the door wide open.

Gavin turned around from the coffee maker. 'Great timing, Michael. How was your journey?' He strode forward, holding out his hand.

'Very good, thank you, Gavin.'

'Have a seat next to Sam. He's giving you a big smile.'

'So I see.' Michael waved at the baby.

'I've made coffee because I got a text from Tina, saying they were on their way back from the shops.' Gavin started taking mugs from hooks.

'Shall I go and say hello to the children and introduce myself to Tom first?'

'Whatever you like. I imagine Tom's probably in need of sustenance by now. I've got mince pies warming if anyone's peckish before lunch is ready.'

He watched Michael go through the back door and grinned at Molly as she brought the sugar bowl to the table. 'Right, Mother-in-law, dear. What's it worth not to say anything about seeing you kissing your boyfriend underneath the Christmas tree?'

'What? Blackmailed by my own son-in-law?' But Molly joined in Gavin's laughter. She'd hardly settled at the table when the back door opened again and Sophie and Jack burst in, bringing a touch of the frosty day with them, their cheeks rosy and their eyes sparkling beneath colourful woollen caps.

Tom followed, Melissa clinging to her daddy's hand. 'Shoes off, children. The girls have just got back and Michael's gone to help them unload the shopping. He seems a nice chap. It'd be great if we could get a round of golf in sometime, the four of us.'

Molly felt her lips twitch. Fifteen love to Michael, even if it was the wrong game.

Tina walked into the kitchen. 'So that's why you're storing up brownie points?'

Michael loomed behind her, holding a Brussels sprout branch. 'Shall I leave this out in the cold?'

'Ooh, yes, please,' said Lucy. 'Fancy you noticing me carrying it while you

216

drove through the village.'

Tom chuckled. 'Not too many people walk around brandishing a Brussels sprout spear, Lucy.'

She made a face at him. 'You know what I mean.'

'Surely you didn't get everything you needed there?' Molly asked.

'No, Mum,' said Tina. 'We went to the superstore first but Mrs Halliday tipped us off about fresh veggies, so I emailed our order to her and she arranged for us to pick everything up this morning.'

'This whole operation's been master-minded,' said Molly, watching everyone milling around her, children chattering, grown-ups bantering.

'You noisy lot,' said Helen as she and Chris joined the party. 'We tried the front door and found it on the latch.'

'Oh, that was me,' said Molly, half-rising from her seat.

'We'll close it properly in a bit, Molly. You sit there. And Michael, here's your coffee at last,' said Gavin.

'No one's introduced us, Michael, but this is my wife Helen, and I'm Chris.'

Michael shook hands with them both. 'Molly's sister and brother-in-law. It's great to meet you.'

'We've been inspecting the church,' said Helen. 'It's beautiful inside.'

'We bumped into the vicar,' said Chris. 'He told us a bit about its history and he also said everyone's welcome at the Midnight Mass service tonight.' He looked at his wife. 'We're definitely going to attend.'

Molly looked at Michael. She didn't think they'd discussed their beliefs whether religious or political. It was a bit late now, if she suddenly discovered they were at opposite ends of the spectrum.

'Sophie might just about make it,' said Tina, who was looking after the children's drinks. 'What do you think, Gav?'

'I'm not sure. But there's enough of us to sort out babysitting so those who really want to attend can do so.'

Molly met Michael's gaze. He gave a

little nod. 'We'd very much like to go,' she said.

'Me too,' said Lucy. 'But I'll babysit if you want to go, Tom.'

'Why don't you all go while Gavin and I stay here?' Tina lowered her voice. 'If we're introducing the little ones to the pool this afternoon, I think Sophie should go to bed at the usual time tonight. Hopefully they'll all sleep well before the big day.'

'And you four bright sparks can sample the local hostelry a bit later in the week and leave us old fogies in charge,' said Chris.

'You speak for yourself,' said his wife. 'I haven't brought all my bling with me for nothing!'

Molly sat back and thought how much John would have loved this festive family reunion. She had a hunch he'd approve of Michael, although that seemed an odd thing to think. Somehow she found the thought reassuring, although she didn't dare try to think about the future in terms of a second marriage. They hadn't known one another long and she'd barely unpacked her bits and pieces in her new home.

Michael hadn't even had a chance to bring his things in from his car. But Chris was asking him what his next tour commitment was, so Molly deliberately concentrated on what Helen was saying. This time with her family, and with the man who'd come to mean so much to her, was too precious to squander by wondering what might happen next. For the next few days she intended to enjoy everyone's company and treasure every single moment.

*　*　*

The sun still shone so Tom and Gavin insisted their late lunchtime barbecue would go ahead as planned. The older children were ecstatic at the thought of eating outside, and this in itself was enough to fire up Gavin and Tom's joint enthusiasm, even if the stream-lined barbeque took slightly longer to ignite than anticipated. The food was all in the building. Tina and Lucy had purchased dips from the supermarket and Gavin remembered earlier to place potatoes in the range to bake until their jackets were crisp and their insides fluffy.

'Thank goodness for a dishwasher,' said Molly as she and Chris stacked dirty crockery while Helen and Michael gave the kitchen a quick blitz, refrigerating unfinished sauces and leftover salad to use up in sandwiches later.

'We'll probably need a midnight feast to boost us after staying up late,' said Molly.

'It's a long time since I attended one of these services,' said Michael.

Molly noticed a faraway look in his eyes. She couldn't see if she too was guilty of the same look, but she entirely understood. She and Michael stood in that no-man's land halfway between the past and the future. Beneath the excitement of plunging into a very different from usual Christmas, they were both bound to feel nostalgic. Neither meant to hurt the other; far from it. Each wanted and needed to share cherished memories of fun and joy with a much-loved partner.

Suddenly she felt very proud of Michael for being brave enough to join them. How might she feel, if catapulted into such a situation? If their relationship deepened, this situation might well happen — and why shouldn't it? She wanted to meet his children. Wanted them to like her.

14

Time to Talk

The two young families were in the sitting room, watching a Disney DVD. Molly rinsed out the cloth she'd been using to mop the work surfaces and decided the owners of Halliday House really had thought of everything necessary for a full-on family party. She looked up to find her sister gazing at her. Chris and Michael had gone into the games room, where there was another television set.

'You were miles away,' said Helen. 'Shall I make us a peppermint tea while it's all quiet?'

'Lovely.' Molly sank into the rocking chair beside the range. 'Bagsy I sit here.'

'The years seem to fall away, don't they? When we're together like this, I mean.' Helen put the kettle on the hob and sat down near her sister.

'It's strange, isn't it? With you and me, it's like we only saw one another last week when we were teenagers. Yet all around us are people who remind us that can't possibly be true.'

'You've been thinking of John, haven't you?'

'I might've known you'd be able to tell.'

'It's nothing to feel guilty about, my love. You had years of happy marriage and, as you say, your children, their partners and now your grandchildren are living proof of that relationship.'

'I know.'

'I get the impression you're willing yourself to step forward but can't help clinging to the past.'

'How can you say that when I sold the home John and I shared for the best part of twenty years and moved away to Wales?'

'That was a very sensible thing to do, in my opinion. And before you did that, you took yourself off on holiday. Another sensible thing, and very well-deserved.' Helen rose to make the drinks.

'I do like Michael. Very much.'

'Then stop agonising. He obviously thinks the world of you, and no one's going to laugh if you hold hands or give one another a kiss. Just because you're a fifty-something doesn't mean you can't show a bit of affection if you want to. Like you and John used to.'

Molly sat up. 'I worry Michael might be wondering how everyone's comparing him with John. When he arrived it was me who first gave him a kiss rather than the other way around. I knew he wondered whether anyone might be watching and what they'd think.'

'You haven't seen a huge amount of each other, have you?' Helen put two steaming mugs on the table and sat down again.

'Quality time, as everyone seems to call it nowadays? No. We stole some quiet moments when we were in Madeira, but he was working, of course. I think I suspected what was happening after I had that silly accident.'

'I was so relieved to hear you'd made a full recovery.'

'Not half as much as I was!' Molly grinned. 'It wasn't until late last summer that we managed to have a day out together. Best of all was when he offered to drive me from Cornwall to Haverstone. Tina and Gavin put him up for the night so they got to know him a bit then.'

'I think I could just about manage that mince pie I was offered but turned down.' Helen got up again. 'How about you?'

'Go on then.'

They munched for a while in companionable silence.

'So have you and Michael talked to each other about your past? Little but significant memories and the things you miss — you know the sort of things I mean.'

'Oh Helen, we have a bit, but not

that much. To be honest, we haven't had much chance in emails and the occasional phone call.'

'Well, I suggest the pair of you take off somewhere the day after Boxing Day.'

'I think Gavin and Tom are hoping to arrange a round of golf.'

'There'll be enough time for that. You look after Number One.'

Molly grinned. 'You're in big sister mode, I see.'

'Quite right too. Chris and I can clear off somewhere as well. Don't get me wrong — we're loving being here; but if we leave the younger ones to themselves, then when we get back it'll be like we've shaken up an old feather mattress and given it new life.'

'That's an original way of putting it.' Molly hesitated. 'Do you think I should go and see how Michael's getting on?'

'No. Let me go instead. I'll take Chris a cup of tea before he can ask for a coffee, which he shouldn't have, and I'll shoo Michael in here.'

As Molly waited on her own, thoughts whirling, she decided her sister had a good point. It was all very well aiming to live for the moment, but practically impossible if you kept looking back at the past. Maybe doing that was more of a woman-thing. She really didn't know.

Michael appeared in the doorway and she smiled up at him.

'You look very cosy,' he said. 'I hope I'm not intruding.'

'We wondered if you'd like a cup of something, or maybe a mince pie. And that sister of mine can be very bossy, you know.'

He nodded and walked a few paces forward. 'We're a bit on show, aren't we, Molly? Each of us so guarded when we're in company.'

'I know. I'm sorry.' He walked so much closer that if she reached out, she could touch him. That blue-green sweater he wore really did something for his eyes and reminded her of the beautiful Mediterranean Sea.

'Is there room for two in that enormous chair?'

Startled, she blinked.

He took her hands and gently pulled her up from the depths of the rocking chair. He sat down in her place and pulled her onto his lap.

'Goodness!'

'Better?'

She snuggled her head against his shoulder. 'Much better.'

'Excellent. I'm not very good at confessing my feelings, Molly. But in case you're wondering, I'd like to say that I've fallen in love with you.' He huffed air through his lips. 'There. I've said what I've been wanting to say ever since I drove down to Cornwall to collect you.'

'Goodness.'

He chuckled. 'Well, that was a conversation stopper. How about this?'

He tipped her chin upwards with the fingers of one hand and bent his head so their lips met again. This time the kiss deepened with all the sweet tenderness Molly knew they felt for one another. Time truly did seem to stand still and she knew, even if the door burst open, that she didn't want the kiss to end.

When they stopped kissing, he stroked her cheek. 'I haven't even told you how old I am. Well, I'm 57 years of age. I'm single but I'm not a widower.'

'But I assumed . . . '

'I never meant to deceive you, Molly, but I'm not proud of the fact that my former wife found someone else. I suppose, ever since the split, I've taken every tour opportunity I could and I've been avoiding even thinking about another relationship with a woman. The truth is, I was still hurting. Still wondering what I might have done to prevent my marriage failing. Until you walked into my life.'

Molly felt breathless. She tried to think of something to say but everything seemed trite. All she could be was honest. 'It's inevitable a lovely man like you would feel like that.'

'I don't know about lovely! To be fair, I think after the children left home, my former wife couldn't handle all those absences caused by my work schedule.'

Molly turned her head to look at him. 'One or two of the women on the Madeira holiday thought you looked like Richard Gere.'

'Are you quite sure it wasn't George Clooney?'

She giggled. 'The general opinion was that you must be married. For a while, I think Kathy hoped I might get together with the other George.'

'Let me think. Ah, I know the one you mean.' He hesitated. 'He was far too old for you.'

She burst out laughing. 'I hope I made it clear I wasn't looking for a husband. I'd have gone on one of those singles holidays if I'd had that in mind.'

'Would you now? So, dare I ask if one day you might change your mind on that score?'

'You mean going on a singles holiday?'

'You know precisely what I mean.'

'I really am hopeless at this sort of thing.'

'You worry too much. Take your time. It's rather pleasant here like this. In fact . . . ' He kissed her again before murmuring, 'I could become accustomed to it.' Still Molly hesitated. Michael said nothing. Only stroked her hair.

Until the door burst open and Jack, who Molly imagined must have escaped the grown-ups' combined eagle eyes, ran into the room. He took one look at his grandmother, turned around and scampered out again.

Molly heard him yell, 'Mummy! Dad! Nana's sitting on Michael's lap.'

Michael held onto her even more tightly. 'Sshh! Listen.'

She heard a cheer go up from the sitting room. Molly suspected the whistle she heard came from Gavin. 'That's it, my reputation's shattered,' she laughed.

'Maybe not completely. Will you marry me, Molly?'

'Yes, please, Michael.' Once the words were out, she could have cheered along with the others.

Gently he tilted her so she stood upright on the colourful kitchen rug. He got to his feet as easily as if little Melissa had been sitting on his knee.

They kissed once more, then walked hand in hand out of the kitchen, across the hallway and into the sitting room.

15

Christmas Bells

The bells of St Peter's rang clear in the frosty air as three couples emerged from the track leading to the village. In a dark velvet sky, stars glittered around a perfect crescent moon. The temperature was a nose-nipping one, but everyone had dressed for warmth rather than style. Inside, the ancient church radiated goodwill as people gathered for worship at this very special time of year. The smell of candle wax, evergreen branches and winter jasmine hit Molly's nostrils, bringing poignant memories of past Christmases.

'It's beautiful,' she breathed, taking Michael's arm as they followed the others.

'I think it's a good job we came early,' he said.

Yet good-natured local people who, Molly suspected, knew exactly who the little band of strangers were, squeezed together in two of the pews near the rear of the church, so the newcomers could be seated.

Molly sank down onto the oak bench, closed her eyes and sent up a little prayer of thanks. When she peeped at him, Michael was still sitting with his head bowed. She still couldn't quite believe he'd asked her to be his wife. But she'd put her doubts behind her and felt convinced they'd both made the right decision.

She gazed at the altar and its surroundings, mellow brass and dark oak shining from years of loving care. A single gold satin ribbon crossed a white cloth, stark as a snowdrift, upon which stood a pair of gleaming candlesticks containing tall white candles. Around the church, vases of red and white chrysanthemums and trailing ivy stood upon windowsills. Evergreen sprigs dotted with bright scarlet holly berries and tied with gold and silver ribbons decorated the ends of pews.

Molly glanced around her, admiring the stained glass of the windows with its vivid blue birds, red and yellow flowers and butterflies, and verdant green foliage. How wonderful it was to be here on Christmas Eve, with her nearest and dearest either close by, or in Tina and Gavin's case, busy at home, stuffing tangerines into the toes of stockings and sorting out tiny gifts to fill up the rest of the space, including ones brought with love by the man who sat beside her, the man who she now knew would one day become her husband.

Suddenly the discreet buzz of conversation came to a stop. The organ music faded to nothingness, but soon the clear voice of a young chorister soared around the church. People got to their feet as the boy sang the first line of 'Once in Royal David's City'. This congregation, and similar ones all over the world, were celebrating the birth of a tiny baby, an infant whose arrival transformed a humble couple into a holy family.

Michael turned his head to smile at her. She nodded and smiled back at him. Meeting him had turned her life around. It had caused her to ask questions of herself. She'd prayed for, and knew she'd found, the right answers.

The service progressed. Congregation and choir responded to the atmosphere of hope and thankfulness. As she sang, Molly thought back to former Christmases, some better and brighter than others. This one would certainly hold a special place in her memory bank. Startled, she realised just how pleasant a tenor voice her new fiancé possessed.

At the end of the service the three couples made their way towards the door, where Molly was first to shake hands with the vicar.

'A little bird tells me you're all staying at Halliday House. It's lovely to welcome you,' he said. 'Where do you live?'

'Just outside of Haverstone in west Wales.'

'I'm from Cardiff,' said Michael.

The kindly vicar looked a little startled when the others mentioned Pembrokeshire and Newcastle. 'Is this a family reunion?'

'Very definitely,' said Molly, squeezing Michael's hand.

But they didn't find conditions outside quite so warm and welcoming. They walked back with extreme caution, Tom shining a torch so the powerful beam would highlight icy patches. Molly noticed he kept his arm firmly around Lucy's waist. She clung to Michael's arm but nobody slipped, and soon they turned in through the gates, which Chris closed behind them. The porch light radiated a welcome pool of brightness as they approached.

In the hall, coloured fairy lights glittered a welcome. Gifts wrapped in shiny paper and tied with gold, silver, green and red ribbons were piled beneath the tree. Everyone hung their coats, hats and scarves on the hallstand and headed for the kitchen to be greeted by the spicy scent of mulled wine. Tina and Gavin sat at the table, listening to music on the CD player. Molly recognised a John Rutter compilation that was a favourite of hers.

'Good service?' Gavin filled the first glass.

'Glorious,' said Helen. 'Ooh, thanks, Gavin. Yes, friendly folk and beautiful decorations. This part of the world is so blessed. One part of me is thrilled to be comfortably off and enjoying myself — the other's sad for those who are cold and lonely and hungry tonight.'

Molly bit her lip. 'It doesn't do any harm to stand back and think like that. It makes us count our blessings.'

'I agree,' said Michael.

She smiled at him, linking her fingers in his. 'I hope I'm not speaking out of turn here, but Michael told me on the way back. Because no one would hear of him contributing towards our family get-together, he wrote out a cheque and handed it to the vicar.'

Michael, looking very embarrassed, cleared this throat. 'Well, as Molly has blown my cover, I can tell you I asked him to split the amount between his church fund and whatever charity they're currently supporting.'

'What a brilliant thing to do,' said Lucy as she took a container of milk from the fridge. 'Would anyone else like a hot chocolate?'

But it was Gavin's mulled wine that everyone else favoured. Molly had her own theory about her daughter-in-law's choice of nightcap but kept her thoughts to herself.

They left the kitchen light on and took their drinks to the sitting room, where the fire made a welcome glow behind the metal guard. Both Molly and Helen, unbeknown to each other of course, had brought with them greetings cards they'd received. These added a special reminder of family and friends to the room, as did the four bulky stockings lying on the carpet at a safe distance from the hearth.

Molly looked around at the familiar faces of her loved ones. 'We really must take some photos tomorrow. I brought my camera but I keep forgetting to do anything with it.'

'We should take an engagement picture of the happy couple,' said Gavin. 'But maybe not while I'm drinking my second glass of mulled wine.'

'We took photos of the children in the swimming pool. They've come out really well. I'll email you all copies after we get home,' said Lucy.

'As for the food, I think we've done everything we should have by now.' Tina snuggled deeper into her corner of the settee. 'I'll put the turkey in the bottom oven before we go to bed and it can stay there all night.'

'Good idea,' said Molly, seated on the settee opposite. 'You probably won't get a lie-in tomorrow, though.'

'I think it's tomorrow now,' said Chris. He raised his glass. 'Happy Christmas, everyone.'

'Happy Christmas,' everyone echoed.

Michael put down his glass and looked at Gavin and Tom. 'Shall we get this show on the road?'

'Crikey, yes,' said Gavin. Michael got up and left the room.

Molly noticed several bemused faces gazing after him. She didn't have a clue what was going on either but noticed her son had his camera at the ready.

'What are you boys up to?' Helen asked.

'You'll see,' said Tom, grinning.

All eyes focussed on the door as a tall white-bearded figure dressed in red jacket, matching trousers and Santa hat walked into the room. He carried a bulging sack over one shoulder and headed for the fireplace, where he knelt beside the filled stockings.

Tom began taking photographs from two or three angles. Michael untied his bag and pretended to extract a gift. Molly saw the sack contained a load of multicoloured, inflated balloons.

'Take a sip of milk?' Gavin suggested.

Michael obeyed. 'I'll put the carrots in my pocket. My reindeer will appreciate them.'

'That's great, Santa,' said Tom. 'You can ride off on your sleigh now.'

But as Father Christmas got to his feet again, the kitchen smoke alarm began to wail.

Tom was first through the door, speedily followed by Gavin and Tina.

'Goodness,' said Molly. 'Surely Gavin didn't leave the mulled wine on the heat.'

'Definitely not,' said Lucy.

'You look tired, darling,' said Molly. 'I hope to goodness we don't have to make a speedy exit.'

'I'm fine, thanks.' Lucy looked down at her hands.

'I won't go rushing in there. Just in case one of the children comes down.' Michael walked towards the settee where he'd been sitting with Molly and stood behind it.

The awful but necessary racket stopped as abruptly as it began.

'Phew. Good job Mrs Halliday showed us where to switch it off,' said Lucy. 'I think I'll go and check on the little ones in case anyone's woken up.'

'Hopefully not,' said Molly, just as Gavin appeared in the doorway with his elder son in his arms.

'I only wanted to make toast for Santa.' Jack buried his face in his dad's neck.

Molly glanced over her shoulder and discovered Michael had dropped out of sight behind the settee. She daren't catch her sister's eye for fear of giggling, so she focused upon Gavin and Jack.

'That was a very kind thought, darling,' she said. 'We know you didn't mean any harm, but I think Daddy would like to put you back to bed now.'

'Night-night, everyone,' said Jack, waving a hand. 'Night-night, Father Christmas.'

Gavin bore his son off back to bed. Tina and Tom came back into the room.

'All clear,' said Tina. 'You can come

out now, Mr Claus.'

Michael appeared from behind the settee, a rueful expression on his face.

'I could quite fancy a piece of toast, actually.'

'NO WAY!' everyone shouted.

16

The Big Day

Molly was first down next morning. She'd put on a bright red sweatshirt over black leggings, ready to do her share of work. She entered a kitchen full of the savoury aroma of roasting turkey but didn't intend interrupting any of her daughter and daughter-in-law's routine. She planned to set the table for breakfast, make a pot of tea and leave the coffee machine to some-one else, as her skills didn't extend beyond knowing how to operate a cafetiere.

Tom was next down. He came into the kitchen and gave his mother a big hug. 'Happy Christmas, Ma. I'm really pleased for you and Michael.'

'I was so afraid . . . '

'I understand that. But I like him and I think you'll be perfect for one another.'

'Thank you,' she said. 'I hope so, but it's been a bit of a whirlwind. We haven't even discussed where we'll live eventually.'

'Well, you each have a house. You don't have to rush into a decision, do you?'

'I suppose not.'

'When are you planning on marrying?'

'Michael's very keen to tie the knot next spring, but I can't think we'll be making much fuss over it.'

Tom chuckled. 'You obviously haven't included Lucy and Tina in that line of thinking.'

Molly gazed at him as he pottered around, giving the teapot a stir and foraging for a biscuit. He'd always loved dunking rich tea biscuits when he was a little boy.

'Tom . . . '

'Yes . . . ' He ran his left hand through his hair, another childhood habit his mother recognised. 'You've guessed, haven't you?'

Molly swallowed hard. 'I hadn't seen her for a while of course, but I can't help noticing little things.' She watched a huge beam of pride and delight flood her son's face.

'We were going to announce our happy news yesterday before church, but we didn't want to steal your thunder. I think both Lucy and I each said a little prayer of gratitude last night though.'

Molly gasped as Tom took her in his arms and waltzed her around the kitchen. She collapsed, giggling, into a chair and demanded tea.

Tom placed a mug before her. 'You know Michael asked my opinion as to whether you might be ready to accept his proposal?'

'I had no idea.' Molly felt tears welling. She blinked hard. 'I know Christmas is an emotional time, but this is getting ridiculous. Could you pass those tissues, Tom?'

'Here you go, Ma. I thought I'd better tell you. It says a lot about the guy, don't you think? He's impressed me, anyway.'

'Good. Did he tell you he's divorced?'

She held her breath. Tom was so like his dad — so traditional, and a firm believer in loyalty and commitment.

'He did. But he didn't slag off his wife, I'm pleased to say.'

Molly frowned.

'Sorry, Ma. I know you dislike that expression. I'm only saying he didn't make excuses for a failed marriage. He expressed only sadness about the effect it might have had upon his two children.'

'At least they're grown up but yes, it must have been dreadful for them all.' Molly sipped her tea. 'We're hoping to arrange for me to meet them as soon as possible. Paul doesn't live far from him but Becca's up north, the other side of the country from you, with her partner.'

'So when do you think we should break our own good news?'

'How far along is Lucy?'

'Fourteen weeks.'

'You'd never know from looking at her, bless her. Why don't you announce your glad tidings when we sit down to lunch? Then no one will wonder why

Lucy's avoiding alcohol. I noticed how she made herself hot chocolate last night when we were all knocking back mulled wine.'

'Not before?'

'Of course, before! There's a kind of look that's hard to describe. I noticed the packets of ginger snaps — another giveaway.'

'Go on, Miss Marple!'

'You were so protective of her on the way home from church — making sure she didn't slip on any icy patches. I'm not sure anyone else noticed. Certainly Helen hasn't said anything.'

'Thanks, Mum. Now do I detect the thunder of tiny feet?'

'It's about time,' said Molly. 'You must have seriously worn out those little ones in the pool yesterday afternoon.'

'Except for Jack!' Tom stood up. 'I'll take my tea with me and keep an eye on proceedings.'

'Have you two said anything to Melissa about her new baby brother or sister?'

'Yep. Lucy has mentioned it but I'm not sure how much Melissa's taken on board.'

'It's good that you've told her. You'll always be able to remind her how she was the very first one to know there was a baby brother or sister on the way. Nice one, Tom.'

Molly thought the children's excited squeals must have roused everyone in the house. She hid the biscuit barrel just in time as Tina and Gavin arrived with little Sam, who was making clear his need for breakfast. Helen followed and mugs were filled with tea or coffee while Molly placed croissants and a few bread rolls in the warming oven.

When she put her head around the sitting room door, she saw Tom was making good use of his video camera as the children opened their presents. Tina brought Sam in and he sat on his mum's knee, chewing a rusk, while his big sister helped him open his own gifts. Jack appeared to have no ill effects resulting from his adventure in the small hours.

Shiny rainbow bubbles were blown, toy cars were pushed around on the carpet and Melissa, with all the determination of a three-year-old, found her way into a chocolate Santa, until Tom carried out a rescue operation and distracted his daughter with something inedible but noisier.

Molly knew she'd be seeing plenty of her grandchildren throughout the day as well as later receiving a copy of the video to enjoy. She was relishing the feeling of being at the hub of things, watching Tina check on the turkey which had turned a lovely shade of golden brown and which smelled wonderful to everyone except poor Lucy, who sat nursing a ginger tea and nibbling a ginger snap.

Helen winked at Molly.

'All right you two,' said Lucy. 'I guess my secret's no longer a secret. I think it's probably only Uncle Chris and Michael who haven't guessed.'

'And maybe Gavin.' Molly chuckled. 'Tina says he's amazingly perceptive of body language and how the people he works with are feeling, but you could be six months pregnant, Lucy, and he might possibly ask Tina if she thought you were putting on a bit of weight.'

Michael walked into a kitchen full of laughter. Chris wasn't far behind him. 'Happy Christmas, everyone, although we've said it already.' Michael bent and kissed Molly on the forehead, placing his hands on her shoulders. She reached up to pat his hand.

'Thank you so much for my gift,' she said. 'I opened it as soon as I woke this morning. It's beautiful, Michael.'

'It's something I brought back from Quebec. It was intended as a friendship gift, but little did I know.'

Tina raised her voice above the laughter. 'So, what is it?'

'An enamelled brooch in the shape of a rose. I shall put it on when I change for Christmas lunch. Now, I wonder if there's any chance whatsoever of those little people eating some breakfast — or are we to turn a blind eye and pretend

chocolate's better for them than porridge?'

★　★　★

Thank you for the world so sweet,
Thank you for the food we eat.
Thank you for the birds that sing,
Thank you God for everything.

Uncle Chris recited the traditional
children's blessing with a little help
from Sophie. By half past one, the family
were gathered around the kitchen table.
The unanimous decision was to leave
setting the dining room table until next
day, for a grown-ups' Boxing Night
dinner to be served after the children's
bedtime. So, toys and books were on
the floor under the table and around
the room with everyone warned to be
careful where they trod.

'You've made a sprout mountain on
Michael's plate, Nana,' said Sophie as
everyone began spooning vegetables
from tureens.

254

'Do you think he'll manage to eat them all?'

'If he doesn't, you could make sandwiches for all the grown-ups, later.'

'I'm sure they'd be thrilled, Sophie. Now, how about a few carrots and peas to go with that one lonely sprout?'

Molly served her granddaughter and turned to Michael. 'I knew it would be chaos,' she muttered. 'But I'm loving every minute.'

Michael nodded. 'These sprouts really are delicious. Crunchy instead of the sad, soggy ones I've been known to produce.'

'These are Mum's speciality,' said Tina. 'She stir-fries them with a little garlic and a sprinkling of flaked almonds.'

'Don't praise her too much,' said Tom. 'You might find them turning up again for breakfast.'

Molly joined in the laughter. 'He's feeling brave because he's not sitting close enough for me to kick him,' she said. 'And it's all right, children, I wouldn't really do such a thing.' She gave her son a hard stare.

'Mmmm,' said Helen. 'This turkey's scrumptious. Falling off the bone but moist and delicious.'

'I'm glad now that we asked Mrs Halliday to order us a locally reared one.' Tina helped her youngest navigate his food. 'That's right, Sam, into your mouth, not your chin. Good boy!'

Gavin picked up his glass. 'We need to drink a toast to the cooks.'

'Any excuse,' Lucy teased him as they all picked up their wine glasses.

Tom glanced at her tumbler of sparkling elderflower cordial. 'And now if I may suggest a second toast, please join me and drink to the health of my lovely wife. Lucy is expecting our second child early next July.'

Molly looked around at the faces. The children were intent on either eating their food or pushing various bits around their plates. The adults' faces all showed their pleasure at the announcement but, she realised, it was only Gavin, Michael and Chris who hadn't guessed; or if they had, they were keeping quiet about it.

'It's wonderful news,' said Michael. 'Have you managed to keep it a secret from everyone?'

Lucy smiled at him. 'As you might expect, Michael, my eagle-eyed female family didn't take long to suss me out. I'm pleased to say I'm absolutely ravenous after a slow start this morning and I'm definitely eating for two — or even three!'

'Do you have twins on either side of the family?' Gavin asked.

'Not on ours,' said Molly.

'I don't think there are any on my side,' said Lucy. 'Just one healthy babe will do us fine. And in case anyone's wondering, we've elected not to know whether it's going to be another little girl or a bouncing boy.'

Tom and Michael exchanged a glance across the table and both rose to top up people's glasses.

'You must be thrilled to bits,' said Michael as he reached his brand-new fiancée's glass. 'I'd love some grand-children.'

'You must share mine,' said Molly.

'Especially when they're being naughty,' said Tom.

'You can be Grandpa Michael,' said Molly.

The banter and laughter continued until it was time to unveil the Christmas pudding. Tina and Lucy were in charge of this, and Gavin and Michael cleared plates from the table while Sophie and Jack went off for a toilet break and Melissa ploughed on with her dinner.

'She's exactly like her father used to be,' said Molly to no one in particular.

'I still eat up all my dinner,' said Tom, looking fondly at his daughter.

Molly was thankful now that she'd made three puddings this year. One was safely at home in her kitchen, having survived the move from Cornwall. The other two were waiting in the warming oven.

'We cheated with the custard,' said Tina, placing a jug on the table. 'This is one produced by a well-known super-market. But the brandy sauce is homemade.'

'We also have double cream.' Lucy carried a glass jug to the table.

'Mum, would you like to start slicing the first pudding?'

'I hope it doesn't fall apart.'

'It'll still taste delicious. I can tell by looking at it,' said Michael. 'What a treat.'

'I'll cut normal-size portions and if anyone wants seconds, we'll start on the other one,' said Molly.

The children were served ice cream, though Sophie tasted a little of her grand-mother's pudding. The men all asked for second helpings, demolished them and promptly decided that a round of golf would be a must and should be arranged at the first opportunity.

'I'm sure there's something about it in the folder they left us,' said Lucy. 'You'll need to ring the golf club tomorrow.'

'Unless it snows,' said Gavin.

'Are you serious?' Aunt Helen asked. 'We might have a sprinkling tomorrow, according to the forecast.'

'Can you play if there's snow on the ground?' Molly asked innocently. She looked around in amazement as everyone dissolved into laughter. 'Oh, all right,' she said. 'Very funny. I was thinking golf balls were that bright yellow, like tennis balls.'

'Come to think of it, Molly, you're on the right track. I watched a television feature a while back, about people in Greenland playing golf. They'd constructed a course alongside a frozen fjord.'

'Thank you, Chris,' said Molly. 'And I bet they use brightly coloured golf balls?'

'Red or orange, from what I can remember.'

'We stand corrected, Ma,' said Tom. 'All the same, I hope we won't wake up to a white world tomorrow.'

'Spoilsport,' said his sister. 'Think of the fun we'd all have making snowmen.'

'Okay,' said Gavin. 'I'll make tea or coffee for anyone who wants one.' He caught his daughter's eye. 'I don't think anyone will mind if you want to get down now, Sophie and Jack. I'm very proud of you.'

Tom gave a little clap. 'Great stuff, you two. Sophie, could you bear to take Melissa with you?'

'I could put a DVD on, if you like,' said Tina. 'While the grown-ups recover. I'll take Sam.'

'I'll come and relieve you in a bit,' said Gavin.

'That was a fantastic meal,' said Michael. 'Thank you so much, all of you.'

'You're very welcome,' said Tina.

Molly noticed her daughter didn't meet Michael's eyes but picked up Sam and headed for the door. 'We'll wash your face and hands, I think, little guy.'

'I'm happy to do some clearing up,' said Michael, 'while you all relax.'

'Why don't we all relax and allow our food to go down, as our mother used to say?' Molly looked at her sister.

'Except we could hardly wait to leave the table once the pudding was eaten,' said Helen. 'The contents of our stockings were far more exciting.'

'Where were you two brought up?' Michael asked.

'In Surrey,' said Helen. 'Not far from where Chris and I live now. Molly of course defected to Cornwall years ago.'

'I'm feeling as if I'm a nomad these days,' said Molly. 'Cornwall, Madeira, Cornwall again, then Wales, and now Gloucestershire in quick succession.'

'And what a brilliant idea this is. Well done, Gavin,' said Chris.

'Tina and Lucy did most of the masterminding.'

'It was a joint effort,' said Lucy. She yawned. 'Would anyone mind if I went for a lie-down? I can hardly keep my eyes open.'

'Of course no one will mind,' said Molly. 'As soon as you come down, I think the grown-ups could open their presents. And we mustn't forget the Queen's speech. I always think it sounds better heard at the traditional time.'

Lucy left the room. Tom glanced out of the window. 'There's not much daylight left. Maybe I'll have a swim later. Burn some calories.'

'Well I think we should play silly games in a while.'

Tom groaned. 'Not charades, Ma, please!'

'You should be good at this kind of thing, Michael,' said Helen. 'I expect you've organised party games for holidaymakers?'

He grinned. 'Not for some years. I still organise quizzes from time to time.'

'Now that sounds a better option. Whenever we play that miming game at Christmas, I haven't heard of half the films and books our children know,' said Chris.

'I just happen to have a couple of quiz books with me,' said Michael.

'We can have two teams.'

Someone's mobile phone trilled. 'Saved by the bell,' said Gavin.

'It's mine. I'm so sorry.' Helen rose and walked towards the door, greeting her caller on the way.

Molly smiled. 'How lovely for her. But our dear mum would've had forty fits if anyone had taken a call while we were at the table. Meals were only interrupted by the outbreak of war or the imminent landing of little green men.'

'Our telephone was on the hallstand,' said Michael. 'I don't think it got much use back then.'

'I wonder when Sophie will decide she wants her own phone,' said Tina.

'Not for ages, I hope,' said Gavin. 'Though I can't imagine it'll be much longer.'

'They can be very useful and they can be a pain,' said Molly. 'Invaluable for keeping in touch though. Chris, do you think your son has proposed to his girlfriend?'

'Two engagements in one family this Christmas? We'll have to wait and see.'

Helen appeared in the doorway

again. 'Chris! Come and speak to Dave. He has something to tell you.'

Molly took one look at her sister's face and nodded. That made two engagements and a happy coming event for Lucy and Tom. Not bad at all for one Christmas.

17

Footprints in the Snow

On Boxing Day morning, Molly and Michael set off through the village to explore a footpath Chris had discovered on the Ordnance Survey map. After breakfast they left the others to play table tennis or run around outside with the children or, in Tom's case, to enjoy a quick swim.

'I'm not sorry to lose those sub-zero temperatures,' said Molly.

Michael tucked her arm in his as they walked down the drive. 'It could of course mean snow's more likely, now the temperature's dropped.'

'I think you're secretly hoping for it.'

'The little ones would enjoy it. But we wouldn't want too much, especially as we get towards the end of our stay.'

'Oh, don't even think about that. I'm

so enjoying myself.'

'So am I.'

'But neither of us has talked about our future,' she said quietly.

'I didn't think it was appropriate to bring up the subject. After I popped the question, there was the church service and my Santa performance, then along came one of the best Christmas Days I've ever experienced. And now here we are, on our own at last.'

She squeezed his arm. 'You realise I have lots of sorting out to do in my new home.'

'Of course. You were hardly there five minutes before you had to travel here.'

'And I have no idea when your next trip is.'

'Ah. Well, in early February I'm escorting a group of people to a favourite place of yours.'

'Funchal again?'

'Yes. I only wish I could take you with me, but . . . '

'It's your job. I do realise that, Michael, envious as I might be.'

'After we're married, we might be able to sort something out. Otherwise, we'll have to wait for a suitable gap between my trips and I can take you somewhere you've always wanted to visit. Does that sound good?'

'That sounds perfect.'

'And I think we should decide where and when we're getting married as soon as possible so all the family can mark the date on their calendars.'

'I've no idea about a venue,' said Molly. 'Maybe you'd like it to be Cardiff?'

'That would be very convenient in many ways, and I gather there are lots of options available.'

'We'd have to marry in a registry office but we could have a church blessing — if you agree, that is.'

'Of course I agree.' He kissed her cheek. 'But we could marry in a hotel that's licensed for marriages, don't forget. That way, we could hold a small reception without having to drive off somewhere else. Maybe Tina and Gavin could help check out suitable places.'

'I'm sure they would.'

Michael looked at her. 'Molly . . . you don't sound too sure. What's troubling you?'

She stopped walking. 'I'm sure about marrying you. I'm just a little worried about Tina.'

He nodded. 'I can't help noticing she's a bit distant with me, but I put it down to having her mind on so many things. She and Gavin have done most of the organising for this get-together.'

'I think it's more than that.'

'You don't think she's had second thoughts about my suitability? Or whether I'm a poor substitute for her father?' He sounded anxious.

Molly put her arms around him. 'I don't care what my daughter or anyone else thinks. I'm giving you a hug because I want you to know how much I care for you. How much I love you and how much I want to be your wife. If Tina has issues with that, she should have them out with me.' She sighed.

'And I think I know why she's behaving as she is. It's not about you, Michael. I think it's the fact that having helped me go through the house hunting and selling up in Cornwall, she can see me upping stumps again and moving to Cardiff. That's why she's being a bit frosty. I'm not even sure she knows she's doing it.'

'Looks like we've reached the footpath. Shall we go on? Then I can share my idea with you.'

* * *

'Lunch smells great,' Gavin called from the utility room while he sorted out slippers in exchange for children's shoes.

'There's plenty of it. Did you have a good game?' Tina asked.

'We did, thanks. All right, Sophie, off you go now and wash your hands. And you, Jack . . . hold Melissa's hand and take her with you, there's a good boy.'

'Tom and Lucy are in the sitting

room. Thanks for organising something outdoors.'

'What time are we eating?'

'I'll feed the children at half twelve,' said Tina. 'We can have ours when the wanderers return.'

Gavin shot her a sideways glance. 'I take it you mean your mum and Michael.'

'Well yes. Auntie Helen and Uncle Chris are using the pool.'

'I do realise this has been a lot of work for you, sweetheart.' He gave her a hug and snuggled against her back as she checked the pan of simmering rice.

'Everyone's mucking in.' Tina hesitated. 'Even Michael. I couldn't believe he thought to bring that Father Christmas outfit. Those photos are brilliant. And you're amazing, as usual.'

'But?'

'I love being here and I'm sure everyone's enjoying the holiday. But it's the end of an era, isn't it?'

'Tina, this is about Molly, I imagine?'

'Molly and Michael, yes.'

'You seemed to have no problem with him when he stayed. I thought you approved of their relationship. You even said you thought your dad wouldn't have wanted her to spend the rest of her life alone.'

'I did! But I was so looking forward to her moving so we had her near us. Now it's happened, and all of a sudden she's engaged to Michael — and who knows where they'll end up living?'

'He mentioned that he's no intention of whisking her off to a villa in Madeira or Spain or somewhere like that. He enjoys coming back to Britain between his foreign trips.'

'But they'll be a married couple. They'll be making a home together.'

'It'd be a bit odd if they didn't. I imagine you'd prefer your mum's new house to be their home but you suspect Michael would rather remain in Cardiff. You have to admit it's a better place to be when it comes to rail links, though I don't think he ever flies from there. His tours usually start from one of the London airports — or from St Pancras, if it's a rail holiday.'

'Exactly. All of a sudden, something I've wondered about ever since Dad died has happened. If only we'd had a couple of years at least with Mum living close by.'

'I think you're jumping ahead too fast, Tina. Please don't let this ruin your holiday. You've got your girls' day out to look forward to later in the week. If we four guys are playing golf tomorrow, it's only fair you ladies shoot off to Fylechester for some retail therapy and a lunch you haven't prepared yourselves.'

'I know. I'm being silly. I can't seem to help it.'

'Christmas is a thoughtful time of year. It's a bittersweet time for looking back to the past and it's on the verge of looking forward to the New Year. It's understandable you should feel as you do, but I've noticed your mum giving you a worried look from time to time. You're going to have to come clean with her soon, don't you think?'

* * *

The footpath led Molly and Michael in a loop around the village, bringing them back to St Peter's. 'Imagine if our marriage could be blessed here in this wonderful old church,' he said as they paused at the lichgate.

'What a lovely thought. But now we've decided our wedding will take place somewhere in Cardiff, I can't imagine that happening.'

'It's something to think about,' said Michael, rubbing his chin. 'But we should go back for lunch now. We don't want to hold everybody up, and I want to see Tina's face when you tell her I have no intention of removing her mum for the foreseeable future anyway.'

'I think you've come up with the perfect solution,' said Molly. 'Thank you.'

He squeezed her hand. 'No. Thank you for consenting to be my wife and for making me so happy.'

They walked up the lane. Molly had

a spare key with her, just in case everyone had gone out walking too. But as soon as she opened the front door, she heard laughter and chatter coming from the kitchen. She turned to Michael, as he wiped his feet on the mat and followed her inside.

'It sounds like home. I mean, it sounds like the home we'd all like or, if we're very lucky, we can recall from the past.'

'Yes and with any luck, we can stop worrying about Tina worrying about you!'

'Shall we tell them straight away?'

'Why not?'

They hung up their coats and scarves and he followed her into the kitchen.

'We're back,' Molly announced. 'I hope we haven't delayed lunch, darling.'

'Not at all,' said Tina. 'Auntie Helen's still drying her hair after her swim, so we thought we'd get the children started, but we can eat as soon as she comes down.'

Molly moved closer. 'Tina, I shall tell

everyone this when we're all together, but we've been discussing our future.'

'Right.' Tina opened a drawer and took out serving spoons.

'It's a future in which our children, both Michael's and mine, form a very important part.' She paused. 'I have no intention of moving now I've finally got myself a house near you and Gavin.'

Tina raised her eyebrows. 'Really?' She reached for a ladle.

'Really.' Molly smiled, seeing Michael take a seat next to her younger granddaughter. 'For at least a few years, until Michael's ready to give up his job, we're going to keep both our houses. I know that sounds extravagant, but there will be times when he needs to be closer to London than Pembrokeshire is. And there'll be times when I shall be delighted to have somewhere to stay when I visit Cardiff. I do have a couple of friends living there, you know.'

'Oh, Mum, I can't tell you what a relief that is! I was hating the thought of losing you so quickly.'

'Michael thinks you and Gavin might enjoy staying at his house sometimes. We could babysit while you see a show or whatever.' She winked at Tina. 'You might even find there are times when you'd like to be rid of me!' Molly chuckled. 'You and I will probably find it helpful if I don't go looking for a job when you can probably use a hand with child care or cooking.'

Tina put down the big ladle and hugged her mum before she moved over to where Michael sat beside Melissa, telling her a story about a kitten that wouldn't eat her dinner. The other children were listening too, all of them clearing their bowls of soup.

Michael glanced up at Tina and smiled. She smiled back and whispered a thank-you before kissing his cheek. Molly breathed a sigh of relief.

★　★　★

The golfing foursome set off after breakfast next morning, Mr Halliday, a member of the golf club, having arranged a booking. Gavin drove his estate car but only Chris and Michael had their kit with them, and lost no time in teasing Gavin and Tom about the joys of young fatherhood, including how their cars were customised by random toys tucked down the sides of seats and packs of baby wipes spilling from the glove compartment and door pockets.

They teed off after the two younger men hired equipment, Michael and Tom taking on Chris and Gavin.

'I'm very rusty,' Michael said as he waited his turn.

'It's just a friendly,' said Chris, watching his partner whack a ball.

Tom and Michael exchanged glances. Michael had learned enough about Chris to know he took the game very seriously indeed. Gavin seemed to be a natural, though he confessed to spending much more time on the garden than on the golf course.

By the time they reached the sixth

hole, Michael saw he wasn't the only one glancing upwards. The sky had taken on that sullen, threatening tinge that signalled snow.

'We should be okay, weatherwise,' he said. 'We're only doing nine holes, after all.'

'This course is pretty exposed,' said Chris. 'But let's keep going a little longer.'

Only minutes later, the first flakes drifted downwards, the sprinkling soon thickening and becoming heavier.

'You all look like abominable snowmen,' said Gavin, striding off in the direction he'd hit his last ball.

'I'm not sure about this,' Michael muttered to Tom as Chris putted his ball neatly into the hole. 'Whether we should go on playing or not.'

Tom gazed around. 'I can't see anyone else nearby. Maybe we should head back.'

'Or at least ring the clubhouse and ask their advice. After all, none of us knows this area well.'

'Good thinking. I'll do that.' Tom took out his phone, shielding it from the elements.

'No luck?' Michael asked after a while.

'No signal. I think it's time to head back.' He waved to the other two.

★ ★ ★

Molly peered through the sitting-room window. 'I hope the golfers are back in the clubhouse for their lunch. It's snowing like it really means it.'

'Surely they'll have stopped playing? Unless of course it's not snowing where they are.'

'I think I'll ring Tom,' said Lucy. 'I wouldn't bother him, but maybe we should warn the boys the snow's pitching here.'

'I'll go into the kitchen. Tina's tuned the radio into the local station. They're sure to have the latest weather update.'

'Do you really think it's that bad?' Helen asked Molly.

280

'None of us know this area. I think we have to be careful, regardless of the way the men might tease us for fussing.' Molly hurried from the room.

Lucy pulled a face and pushed her phone back in her jeans pocket. 'Nothing. Surely he hasn't switched off his mobile?'

'Could it be the weather conditions causing a problem? No way am I clued up about these things,' said Helen.

'When Tina comes back downstairs with Sam, I'll ask her to try Gavin's phone. That DVD the children are watching seems to be holding their attention. Not one of them has noticed the snow yet.'

'I think I'll fetch my camera. On the one hand, it's worrying, but the garden's already looking magical.'

Before Helen could leave the room, Molly came back. 'Heavy snow forecast to continue for the next few hours in this area. Let's hope the men are on their way back.'

'I couldn't get through to Tom,' said Lucy. 'Which makes me think they're out in it somewhere. Either still on the golf course or driving back through the snowstorm.'

'I'll tell Tina and collect my camera from our room. Shan't be a tick.'

Molly and Lucy stared at one another as Helen left. Molly hated the thought of her daughter-in-law becoming alarmed, even though she felt the same tummy lurching she experienced when waiting for important news or sometimes when she set off on a long drive. Except this time she had her daughter-in-law and four men to worry about.

'We should have something to eat soon. Tina's put the children's macaroni and cheese to warm in the slow oven. Shall I do a few peas?'

'I should be doing that.'

Molly chuckled. 'No way. The rest of us have decided you should take advantage of all the eager helpers around you and grab the chance to put your feet up. While you can!'

'Well, it's much appreciated.'

'Just you stay there. The potatoes are baking in the top oven and I've got turkey slices waiting in the fridge. We can finish off the salad stuff and stock up again tomorrow for the rest of our stay.' Molly kept her voice cheerful, even though her thoughts whirled like the snowflakes dancing outside the windowpane.

★ ★ ★

Fast-falling flakes blinded Michael as he bent his head and pushed on over the snow-covered course. The four men kept close together, hoping they weren't disorientated in a landscape with which not one of them was familiar.

'I can't believe this has disrupted mobile phone reception,' Tom called. 'It may be the signal's weak around these parts anyway.'

'Surely they wouldn't have let us get on the course if they thought there'd be a whiteout?' Gavin suggested.

'This morning when I checked on the

internet, this area wasn't even border-line for snow. I should have used my head and been less trusting.'

'We all wanted to play golf, Tom,' said Chris. 'It's not your fault.'

'I wonder what it's like back in the village,' said Michael.

'Until we get to the clubhouse, we won't know. Even if we can't get a mobile signal, there's a public call box in the foyer.'

Michael decided not to complicate matters by broaching the subject of lines bowed down by heavy snow. He sheltered his eyes with one hand and looked into the distance for signs of the clubhouse. But all he saw was white.

18

A Blessing in Disguise

Back at Halliday House the women sat around the kitchen table with the children. Molly knew everyone, including herself, was trying to steer the conversation away from the weather. Sophie was especially focussed on the possibility of building a snowman.

'I wish I'd taken them for a walk first thing, instead of getting involved with that colouring session,' Tina muttered to Lucy.

'We'll cope. I wondered about doing some baking.'

'It'll have to be something really simple, like chocolate crispies,' said Lucy, while Molly questioned Sophie and Jack about the film they'd watched.

'Definitely. None of us arrived equipped to compete in *The Great*

British Bake Off,' said Tina.

'What, didn't you pack arrowroot and vanilla essence? Freeze-dried raspberry powder and ground almonds?'

'I'd have to check.'

Molly noticed the two giggling and hoped the mood wouldn't deteriorate. Suddenly she wondered if the landline was in working order. If so, she'd ask Tina to look up the golf club's number or check the folder on the hall table. The Hallidays had left a list of numbers, including of course their own. Knowing how organised and friendly the couple were, Molly was surprised they hadn't rung to make sure their holidaymakers were coping all right.

Meanwhile Jack was talking about flying dragons and Sophie was bursting to tell her nana about the princess who got kidnapped. Outside, the snow continued to fall and the trees, Molly decided, looked like American footballers made gigantic by all those layers.

★   ★   ★

'Look!' Gavin pointed. 'There, at one o'clock. What a relief.'

'Phew. I'm almost out of puff. Thank goodness the cavalry's on its way,' said Chris. 'I know this course loops around and brings us back to the clubhouse, but I think we went around in circles for a while there.'

Michael felt a huge sense of relief as he saw the Land Rover, its orange paintwork bright against the white world, battling across the fairway. The four kept walking, but knowing they'd soon be riding back to the warmth of the clubhouse helped increase their pace. He hoped Molly and the others weren't worried about them, but there was always the possibility of this snowstorm being a localised one.

The driver got the four men and their bags bundled into the vehicle and back to base within a few minutes. When they went to the desk to ask about telephoning, the receptionist called to Tom.

'I'm so sorry your visit to us hasn't been enjoyable, Mr Reid. The weather caught out quite a few people.'

'We wondered if we were the only ones daft enough to be out there,' said Tom.

'Not at all. You'd strayed away from the beaten track though.'

'I don't suppose anyone's been trying to get in touch with us?'

The woman shook her head. 'I don't think so. Would you like me to ring anyone while we still have a landline?'

Tom grimaced. 'I don't have the number of Halliday House, I'm afraid.'

'I'll see if it's on our database. If not, I'll try Mr Halliday's home number.'

'That's very kind.' Tom turned to the others. 'Why don't you head for the bar? I'll come and find you.'

'I'll stay here,' said Michael.

The receptionist turned back to Tom. 'We do have the number of Halliday House. I'll try it for you.'

But Tom and Michael waited in vain.

'It's ringing unobtainable,' said the receptionist.

'How are the roads?' said Tom.

'The main road's clear but I gather the side roads are a problem.'

'We need to get back to Coln St Peter.'

'You should be okay to do that, but you might have to leave your vehicle in the village and walk the rest of the way.'

Tom looked at Michael. 'Lunch?'

'Most definitely. And I think we should each of us try his phone and see if we can get through in case they're worrying.'

'As long as they don't try to go out,' said Tom. 'Children can be very persuasive, especially if they're cooped up too long.'

'Don't worry, Tom. I can't imagine any of them setting foot outside in weather like this. Especially Lucy.'

'I'm sure you're right. Now, time for lunch and a mobile phone onslaught.'

★ ★ ★

It was Tina who managed to break through the silence and ring her husband's mobile phone. Gavin picked up the call as his plate of cottage pie and vegetables arrived.

'Thank goodness, Tina,' he said. 'We're all okay and about to have lunch. How about you?'

'Everyone's eaten. Lucy got the log fire going but the heating's fine. We're playing some kind of hide-and-seek at the moment, except Sophie made up the rules and I'm not sure if everyone understands.'

Gavin grinned. 'Least of all you! I'll tell everyone you're having fun, shall I?' Anticipating her indignant reaction, he held the phone away from his ear for a moment.

'We'll set off as soon as we've eaten, love. That way, we can get back in the daylight.'

'Drive carefully, Gav. Mr Halliday trudged along the lane to tell us the main road's still passable but the side roads are a nightmare.'

'Don't worry. I guess the car will tell me when it's time to stop. Talk to you later.' He looked round at the others. 'We'd better eat up and get going.'

But daylight was fading, though the snow had stopped when the four men finally made their way through the back door of Halliday House, stamping their feet and pulling off shoes and boots.

'What a time you must have had! Mulled wine awaits,' said Helen. 'You certainly got more than you bargained for when you booked a session on the golf course.'

Molly and Michael exchanged a hug. 'Promise not to tell any tour guide jokes,' he said.

'I wouldn't dream of it. I'm just relieved you're all back safe and sound.'

'We were lucky to be rescued before things got really nasty. Without landmarks and with hardly any vision, we all got disorientated.'

'You're safe now.'

He looked down at their linked hands. 'I've been hoping I can take you into Fylechester to buy a ring, but goodness knows when we'll get there.'

'You mustn't worry. After all, I'm wearing your lovely brooch.'

'Let's hope the temperature stays above freezing. It's going to be horrendous out there if it doesn't.'

'We've written off our day out.' Molly shook her head. 'One of those things.'

'I've been thinking about that,' said Michael. 'I'm going to suggest we chaps carry out the childcare and cooking duties anyway. You mightn't find the food up to gastropub standards, but we'll make sure you four have a rest from domestic chores.'

Helen overheard. She came closer and put her arm around her sister. 'You've got a good 'un there, Molly.'

'I know.' Molly smiled as she saw Michael shuffle his feet in embarrassment. 'And maybe the snow's a blessing in disguise. We'll have another day of being together. Isn't that what Christmas is all about?'

'Excuse us a moment, please, Helen.'

Molly gasped as Michael took her hand and pulled her after him into the hallway. He pointed upwards.

'It's so high I hadn't noticed it before, but I imagine our hosts must have put it there.'

Molly looked up at the chandelier. 'Who'd have thought it?'

Michael took her in his arms. 'Who'd have thought a trip to Madeira could lead to a new life for us both?'

Molly closed her eyes as her fiancé kissed her beneath the mistletoe.

THE END

We do hope that you have enjoyed reading this large print book.

Did you know that all of our titles are available for purchase?

We publish a wide range of high quality large print books including:
Romances, Mysteries, Classics
General Fiction
Non Fiction and Westerns

Special interest titles available in large print are:
The Little Oxford Dictionary
Music Book, Song Book
Hymn Book, Service Book

Also available from us courtesy of Oxford University Press:
Young Readers' Dictionary
(large print edition)
Young Readers' Thesaurus
(large print edition)

For further information or a free brochure, please contact us at:
Ulverscroft Large Print Books Ltd.,
The Green, Bradgate Road, Anstey,
Leicester, LE7 7FU, England.
Tel: (00 44) 0116 236 4325
Fax: (00 44) 0116 234 0205

CALIFORNIA DREAMING

Angela Britnell

When plucky L.A. journalist Christa Reynolds loses her fiancé and her job, she decides it's time for a change of scene. Nearly seventy years ago, her English-born grandmother was evacuated from war-torn London to safety with the Treneague family in Cornwall, and as there's been a standing invitation ever since for the Reynoldses to visit, Christa decides to take them up on it. But she hadn't reckoned on meeting wounded ex-Marine Dan Wilson, and soon she has a life-changing choice to make . . .

SECRET HEARTACHE

Teresa Ashby

Midwife Emma Finch starts work at a new hospital, the Bob, back in her native Yorkshire. It's supposed to be a fresh start for her and her daughter, Keira, but then she discovers that Nick Logan — the man she once loved with all her heart, and who left her when she needed him most — is her department consultant. It soon becomes clear that the old spark between them is still very much alive. Can Emma and Nick reforge a relationship after the heartbreak of the past five years?

THE FIDDLER'S WALTZ

June Davies

In post-war Liverpool, Ellen Butterworth's ambitious sweetheart Brian leaves the Navy and comes ashore so they can begin a future together. An urgent telegram from her younger sister Jeanette interrupts their wedding plans, and Ellen must return to the Yorkshire wool town where she grew up. Unexpectedly, Brian follows her — he wants them to be married there and then in Yorkshire! But, from the moment Jeanette appears in the room, Brian isn't able to take his eyes from her . . .

THE ORCHID

Lucy Oliver

London, 1840: When Ava Miller's father died, she promised she would continue to run The Orchid Theatre and look after its close-knit family of actors. But when Henry Scott-Leigh, the son of the wealthy owner of the theatre, turns up one day threatening to replace Ava or close the unprofitable business altogether, the future looks bleak. Can Ava make a success of the next play and save everything she loves? And what will come of the growing attraction she and Henry share, when they inhabit such different worlds?